A jaded, reluctant smile cur— — night prince's
lips as Kellen saw him walk toward the dark, sandy
beach through her store window.

How long would it be before she met him? Maybe he
was a rock star? Or perhaps a vampire ... and she
was under his hypnotic spell.

Reluctantly, Kellen went back to work. And then she
heard a faint rap on the window. She felt a tingling
sensation, and as she turned around, she saw her
majestic prince.

As she gazed into his commanding eyes, it occurred
to her that he could rule by virtue of his seductive
smile. He put his fingertips to his lips and blew her a
kiss, his suddenly night-dark eyes lingering on her
like a touch.

Unable to move, Kellen watched him, mesmerized
beyond her own understanding ... and awed that she
had no will of her own.

ABOUT THE AUTHOR

Muriel and her husband, Ron, live halfway up a hill on which Astoria sits at the mouth of the Columbia River. She walks downtown almost every day to share morning coffee with friends at the bakery. One day as she passed her favorite bookstore, Muriel was reminded of a phone conversation she'd had with her niece, who'd just started a commercial window-decorating business. As Muriel thought about her niece at work, inspiration struck, and her romance writer's imagination began conjuring up a heroine for a book! But what would her hero look like? A tall, dark, handsome man formed in her mind—wearing a black coat and an air of mystery. And that's when *Night Prince* began to take shape. The process of character creation is a "serendipitous thing," according to Muriel. She hopes American Romance fans enjoy reading about Kellen Clark and Dominic Hunter in *Night Prince* as much as she enjoyed writing about them!

Books by Muriel Jensen

HARLEQUIN AMERICAN ROMANCE
464—MIDDLE OF THE RAINBOW
478—ONE AND ONE MAKES THREE
507—THE UNEXPECTED GROOM

MURIEL JENSEN

NIGHT PRINCE

Harlequin Books

TORONTO • NEW YORK • LONDON
AMSTERDAM • PARIS • SYDNEY • HAMBURG
STOCKHOLM • ATHENS • TOKYO • MILAN
MADRID • WARSAW • BUDAPEST • AUCKLAND

To Tammy Eldredge, whose creative
Window Works inspired my heroine

ISBN 0-373-16522-6

NIGHT PRINCE

Chapter One

There he was again!

Kellen Clark ducked behind the ornate sleigh and the white fake-fur clad mannequin leaning against it and peered around to watch.

This was the third night in a row that she'd seen the man appear out of the shadows at the east end of Sandpiper's three-block commercial district. Just as he had last night and the night before, he walked slowly down the middle of the two-lane street, looking with interest in all the windows, appearing to drink in the modest glamour of the small coastal Oregon town Kellen was dressing for the holiday season.

He wore a black trench coat, its collar pulled up against the mid-November cold, the end of a long black scarf tossed over his shoulder. His hair, brown or black—she couldn't be sure—blended into the darkness. The night before, when he'd glanced at the window of the bookstore she'd been decorating, she'd taken note of his strong, sinfully handsome Mediterranean features.

From behind her display she'd watched him approach the window and study several of the hardbacks artfully spilled in the mock fireplace she'd created in a corner. A half-sized mechanical Santa proceeded toward a tree at the other side of the window, dropping a trail of books from a hole in his sack.

The man's thickly lashed eyes as black as the night had roved the display. A jaded, reluctant smile curved his lips. Then one of the two burly men who'd also been with him the night before, caught his arm and urged him on. He'd gone without argument toward the dark, sandy beach.

Kellen had thought about him and his mysterious midnight walks for hours. Was he a rock star? she'd wondered. A millionaire? A vampire?

She'd fallen asleep on the woozy decision that he was probably some sort of exiled prince, forced to seek the safety of foreign shores.

As she slipped into dreams, she had imagined his richly accented voice, his regal bow, his dress uniform complete with ribbons of heroism and a sash of office. She had been on his arm, of course, because that was what dreams were made of.

Tonight, the two men were with him again, one nearly as wide as he was tall, the other more slender, and watchful. He held a hand inside the breast of his overcoat. She wondered for a moment if he concealed a gun there.

As they moved past her window, Kellen leaned over the sleigh to watch them proceed toward the beach. She glanced at her watch. It was after midnight.

They disappeared into the shadows beyond Castle Clothes' window, and Kellen went back to work, thinking that the prince interfered seriously with her productivity. She should have been finished by now, and working on the shoe store. But she'd have to save that for tomorrow night. She had an eight-o'clock appointment in the morning with a wholesaler in Portland, which was a ninety-minute drive.

"Such is the lot of a poor working girl!" she told herself philosophically as she walked around the sleigh to the mannequin wearing a full-length fake fox, a hand frozen in elegant grace on the side of the sleigh.

Kellen had draped two filmy scarves over her arm, one silvery gray, the other mossy green. She tried each one on the mannequin. As she stepped back to study the effect of the green one, a rap on the window startled her and caused her to spin around.

It was the prince.

It occurred to her as she looked down into his face that if the nations' armies had been composed entirely of women, he would rule the world by virtue of his smile. It was inviting, suggestive, complimentary and sexy all at once.

The two men were on either side of him. The shorter, wide one caught his arm and tried to pull him away from the window. He said something over his shoulder that made the man argue with him, then finally let him go.

The taller man, hand in his coat, looked around nervously.

The prince took a step closer to the window to point at the gray scarf over Kellen's arm. In the lights, she saw that his hair was black and a little long, shiny as silk, its curly ends caught inside the raised collar of his coat. She felt her pulse grow erratic.

She held up the scarf in question.

He nodded, then pointed to the mannequin, indicating, she guessed, that she should put the scarf on it.

She pulled the green scarf off, replaced it with the gray, then turned to him.

He gave her a thumbs-up, then pointed to the green scarf she now held.

"This?" she said silently, holding it up.

He nodded, then drew a flat circle in the air with his finger.

She shook her head in perplexity.

He drew the circle around his own neck, and when that produced the same confused reaction in her, he removed his own scarf, then put it on again, pointing to the green scarf, then to her.

"Oh!" she exclaimed silently, then draped the scarf around her neck, tossing the silk end over her shoulder and striking a playfully glamorous pose.

He applauded, smiling broadly. Then he seemed to sober somewhat as he pointed his index finger under his eye, then at her.

When he did it a second time, she understood, and felt her own smile sober. He was telling her that the scarf was the color of her eyes.

She wasn't sure why that should wipe the humor from his face, but the fact that it did affected her own.

The stout man said something to him and the prince nodded at him without taking his eyes from Kellen.

Then he put his fingertips to his lips and blew her a kiss, his suddenly sad night-dark eyes lingering on her like a touch.

Before she could think about the action, she put her own fingertips to her lips.

He closed his eyes and placed a hand dramatically over his heart. She laughed. He winked, then with one more longing look at her face, turned to walk down to the beach.

Kellen watched him, touched beyond her own understanding.

DOMINIC HUNTER'S long strides ate up the center line of Main Street as he raised his face to the wind. The night was biting cold and spiked with rain.

"That ain't safe, boss!" Gordy complained, his short legs working doubly hard to keep up, his breathing already labored. "Contact ain't safe! You gotta listen to us."

Spike was walking backward as fast as Dominic was, his eyes ranging the shadows for any sign of trouble.

Dominic kept moving. "She was just a girl, Gordy."

"Girls makes the best hit men 'cause nobody sees 'em coming. Remember Lenny the Clam? A dame did that hit. Shot him right in the back. And Guido Garagiola that took a bullet in the groin in a Pittsburg fancy house, that was—"

Dominic stopped in his tracks, afraid that if he didn't get out from under the protection of Gordy and Spike, and Burton, the security man his agent had hired, he was going to implode.

"Look," he said quietly, putting a hand on Gordy's shoulder. It was thick and meaty under the loud blue plaid suit. "Why don't you guys go home?"

He turned to reason with Spike. "I don't really need you guys. Everybody's making more out of this than is really there. I'll be fine."

Spike, whose eyes never stopped sweeping their surroundings, spared Dominic one swift glance.

"Can't, boss. Your uncle says we're to stay right with you till it's over."

"Okay," Dominic said. "Then, it's over. I'm saying it's over. You're here to protect me and I'm telling you it's over."

Gordy looked at him as though he'd just fallen from the sky. "It ain't over till Rocco says it's over. Me and Spike ain't leaving your side till Rocco calls us home."

"Listen." Dominic placed an arm around Gordy's shoulders, then turned Spike around and led them toward the water. He could hear the quiet surf in the darkness and longed to be on it, heading south on his sailboat. "I know this may come as a surprise to you guys, but my Uncle Rocco doesn't run the world. He doesn't run me."

"He runs the south side of Chicago," Gordy amended. "When you live there, he runs the world."

"But, I don't live there. I live in Connecticut."

"But Spike and me, we live in Chicago. Rocco runs us. He told us to stay with you till it's over and that's what we're gonna do. Besides—" he gave Dominic a slap on the back that nearly collapsed a lung "—we like you."

"That's nice," Dominic replied thinly.

"Rocco told us you wouldn't like being shut up like this, but it's the only way we can keep you alive, you know?"

"We shouldn't even be out walking like this," Spike said. "It ain't safe."

They reached the sand. Dominic kept heading for the water. "Doesn't it bother you guys to be cooped up all day? To never go out?"

Gordy shook his head. "Nah! We done it before. We spent two weeks with Lenny the Clam in a hotel room a lot smaller than the house we got you in."

Dominic caught a detail in that remark that caused him concern. "You were protecting Lenny the Clam? When he got shot in the back by a hit man?"

"Hit *woman*," Gordy corrected. "But that wasn't our fault. He was supposed to stay with us and he wandered off. I know what you're thinking, but me and Spike are good. Lenny got it because he didn't listen."

Lenny got it, Dominic thought, because he probably decided to take his chances rather than spend another moment with Gordy and Spike.

Dominic watched the ruffled waves, their white-caps all that were visible in the darkness of the ocean. He tried to concentrate on the sound to calm himself.

After just a week of the confinement that was supposed to save his life, he was chafing against it so badly he was afraid he was on the brink of doing something stupid.

Only the thought of his sons stopped him. And it wasn't that they needed him so much, it was that he needed them. They were so sharp, so resourceful, so critically important to his sanity that he didn't want to miss a moment of their lives.

He heaved a deep sigh. He had to stay here. He might be able to ditch Gordy and Spike, but every law enforcement agency from the police to the feds were after him, and getting picked up would only complicate an already complicated situation.

He had to be smart. There was too much at stake.

Gordy patted him consolingly on the shoulder. "What would make you happy, boss? Maybe Spike could find it, or maybe Rocco could send it over. Different food, better wine, some Playboy videos?"

Dominic had to smile as he headed up the beach, Gordy straining to keep up with him in the sand, Spike staring out at the ocean as though expecting a water-mounted assault. All Rocco's men needed to be content was junk food, some cold beer, and a big-screen TV to watch sports, game shows, and gory horror movies.

"You know what might take my mind off all this?" he said fancifully, the very thought filling the tedium with new excitement.

"What?" Gordy asked.

"A night with the green-eyed angel in the window."

"Dames are trouble," Gordy scoffed.

Dominic knew that. Betsy had been trouble. And he was convinced there was nothing on this earth to match the experience.

"FANTASY WINDOW WORKS." Kellen cradled the portable phone on her shoulder as she moved around the corner of her kitchen that served as an office.

"Kell, what have you done with the Call Your Mother mug I sent you? You're obviously not using it."

Kellen smiled as she gathered the Christmas decorations she would need for the shoe store window into a box. "Hi, Mom! I use it all the time. If you weren't always globe-trotting, you'd be home when I call. I keep telling you to get an answering machine."

"Then I'd have to return all those calls. That cuts into my roulette time."

Kellen could hear bells and commotion in the background. "Where are you?"

"Tahoe. I'm winning big. How's business?"

"Great. Christmas, you know. Gradually, I'm getting every store window in Sandpiper looking like a Christmas card."

"Glad to hear it. Don't forget to eat red meat once a week, to get your quota of beta carotine, and to floss regularly."

Kellen held the phone away, frowned into it, then replaced it at her ear.

"What's the matter, Mom?" she asked.

"Nothing. Reminding you to take care of yourself is my way of telling you I love you."

Kellen looked thoughtfully at a garland of stars she was about to place in the box. "I know that, Mom. Are you okay?"

"I'm fine," Mary Ellen replied, then heaved a gusty sigh. "I just worry about you, all alone. You should be married and having kids. I should live down the block and run over with cookies and sourdough bread."

Kellen laughed at the image that came to mind. "You can't write travel books from down the street. Besides, I'm not alone. I have lots of friends. And I have Carrot."

As though hearing her cue, a large orange tabby leapt onto the small desk wedged into Kellen's office and flung a twenty-pound body against her mistress's elbow.

Mary Ellen sighed again. "That's why I'm worried, Kell. You actually consider a cat sufficient company. Well…it's a different world from the one I grew up in."

"You never grew up, Mom."

"Don't be smart, darling. Got to go. I'm hot at the blackjack table. I'll be in touch. Love you."

"Love you, too, Mom. Bye."

Kellen palmed down the antenna on the phone, replaced it in its cradle, and shook her head over her mother. She'd been married too young to a wilderness guide who'd swept her off her feet. The reality of life miles away from convenience and companionship had soon destroyed the romance of falling in love with a mountain adventurer.

After the marriage broke up, Mary Ellen took up travel writing and Kellen followed her mother from one vacation spot to another, except when school schedules prohibited. All that globe-trotting had made Kellen a homebody.

But she and her mother loved each other a great deal, though the only time they usually had together was a few days at Christmas.

Kellen went to her tool case under the kitchen table and removed every hammer she owned, then added them to the box. She was about to convert Marshall's Shoes into Santa's workshop.

All her supplies in the van, she went to the hall tree for her serviceable denim coat. Still tucked under its collar was the green scarf from Castle Clothes. She'd left a check for it on the counter the night before.

For an instant her mind was cleared of all the things she had to do tonight, of all the problems and responsibilities that plagued a young woman in business for herself.

She thought only about the prince. As if he stood before her now, she could see his deep, dark eyes, his thick silky hair, and the collar of his coat turned up against his strong jaw. She remembered his smile.

She felt the same stirring of excitement at the memory of what she'd felt last night when there'd been only a window between them.

She frowned over the sadness she'd glimpsed in his eyes. Who was he? she wondered in frustration. And what was he doing in Sandpiper with bodyguards?

Her watch beeped 7:00 p.m. She slipped into her coat as she ran out to the van, putting the prince out of her mind. What he was doing in town was none of her business, and a brief and silent contact through a window in the middle of the night was no cause to turn giddy.

She was a very practical young woman. She had a going business and this was a season that required all her energy and attention if Fantasy Window Works was going to grow even bigger. Fairy tales about princes who went forth only at night were for other women who had time for such things, women with day jobs who were less vulnerable to the seductive suggestions of the night.

Still, before she turned the key in the ignition, she tucked the silky ends of the scarf inside her coat and let herself remember that he'd pointed to its boggy green color, then to her eyes. And there'd been a look in his . . .

She turned the key, the old Dodge van sputtered to life, and she headed off to work, dismissing every thought in her head except those that related to the big double windows of Marshall's Shoes and the elfin workshop she would create therein.

By midnight, Kellen had worked her magic. In one corner of the window, a plump elf pointed with frantic expression to a calendar where the twenty-fourth of December had been circled in red ink.

Gathered around a worktable was a group of elves, each holding one of Kellen's motley collection of hammers. Before them on the table were shoes sold by the store. She showed everything from hiking boots to bedroom slippers, both men's and women's. Glittering evening shoes were being admired under the table by a female elf who was obviously avoiding the frantic pace of the workshop in preference of a little romantic reverie.

As Kellen stepped back to study her work, she wondered if she identified too well with the daydreaming little elf.

The second window depicted an outdoor scene, Santa in front of the workshop, feeding Rudolph while waiting for the elves to finish. At his feet were several stacks of shoe boxes displaying all the brands sold by Marshall's.

She'd used the star garland in the window ceiling over Santa's head to represent the night sky. The glittering effect was the finishing touch.

Kellen stretched her arms and then her back that had grown tight from all the hours of working crouched or bent over. In the big city, she thought, as she gathered up her tools and scraps, the newer stores had tall display windows a dresser could step right into without having to climb in and out like a burglar.

Warren's in Portland had invited her to work exclusively for their eight Pacific northwest stores. She had considered it, lured by the luxury of not having to drive one hundred miles to rent mechanical figures or obtain supplies when she needed them. The security of a steady job she didn't have to hustle for every season of every year had been tempting.

But Sandpiper had won out. She'd visited the town one summer at age eighteen, accompanying her mother as she prepared a travel book entitled *Coastal Curiosities in Oregon,* and she'd fallen in love.

"Are you out of your mind?" Mary Ellen had asked when Kellen graduated from college and announced she was moving to Sandpiper in the fall. "It rains all the time. It's cold in the winter. A community that size can't support the designy things you like to do."

Kellen had hugged her mother and continued making plans. When Mary Ellen wasn't traveling, she loved the fast pace and the sunshine of Los Angeles. Kellen longed for quiet, small-town life and a sense of permanence her childhood had never provided.

In the end, Mary Ellen had loved her enough to send her on her way with her blessing.

Kellen looked out at the black night beyond the window and the lights in the other festive windows she'd decorated up and down the street. In the midnight quiet she could hear the surf down the street, and the occasional whoosh of a car passing on the highway up the hill. She did not regret her decision for a moment. She had friends, and a business that indulged her artistic inclinations and made her and other people happy. She couldn't imagine life had anything better to offer.

She had a brief mental flash of dark brown eyes and a disarming smile. Where was he tonight? she wondered. She hadn't seen him. But she didn't allow herself to linger over thoughts of him. She'd never done very well with men, anyway. She thought it was because she was too straightforward for the games they liked to play.

Kellen made several trips to the van with her cleaning supplies and tools. The street was well lit but deserted. Sandpiper was a town in which crime was usually relegated to vandalism and the drunk and disorderly conduct of teenagers who'd partied too long on the beach.

But she worked quickly and kept her key chain with its tube of Mace in her hands at all times. The interstate was just a few blocks away, and though she trusted everyone in Sandpiper, she was as careful as a single woman should be about strangers.

On her last trip to the van, pulling on her coat, she stopped in the middle of the sidewalk, unable to dispel the feeling that she was being watched. She turned at the sound of a footstep, only to find nothing behind her but Marshall's. She shook her head over her own susceptibility to suggestion as she walked around to the driver's side.

Everyone in his right mind was in bed at this hour. It occurred to her that it wasn't people in their right minds she should be worried about.

She chuckled to herself at the thought. The next moment, as she fitted her key in the lock, she choked on the chuckle as a hard hand clamped over her mouth, and another around her waist dragged her backward.

Chapter Two

For an instant, Kellen was too shocked and terrified to react. Then anger took over and she struggled for all she was worth.

"Hey, hey!" A voice whispered in her ear. "It's okay. We're not gonna hurt you. Just be still. Be still!"

Somewhere in her mind Kellen accepted that she wasn't able to free herself. The arms that held her were simply too strong. But when panic tried to take hold of her, she continued to struggle. It seemed important that whoever held her think she believed in herself.

"Easy. Easy!" the voice whispered. "Calm down. You're going to hurt yourself."

Had Kellen been able to bite through the hand over her mouth, she'd have taken pleasure in telling him that what she did to herself would be nothing compared to what she intended to do to him the moment she had the chance.

As she struggled against the man holding her, she heard a car door open and felt her legs lifted by a second man as she was swung headfirst and facedown into the back seat.

"We're not going to hurt you," a voice whispered again and her hands were tugged behind her back and tied there. She tried to turn to see her attacker, but before she could focus something soft and smelling of laundry detergent was tied over her eyes.

"You're hurting me now!" she cried angrily, struggling to keep the fear from her voice. "Let me go this instant!"

Now something was drawn swiftly and tightly over her mouth and tied at the back of her neck, though her captor was careful to see that she could breathe.

A door was closed, another opened. She heard the sound of fabric sliding along upholstery, doors closing. She shouted indignantly behind the gag.

"Just quiet down, little lady," the voice said. "Everything'll be fine. You'd better step on it, Spike."

A motor roared to life and the car was launched from its parking spot. Only the quick jut of her foot against the back of the front seat prevented Kellen from rolling onto the floor.

She screamed loudly and continuously under the gag, the sound feeble and useless. She finally lay quietly against the cold upholstery, regrouping.

She guessed they had driven about fifteen or twenty minutes when the car stopped. She heard a garage door open and close. Anger receded and fear grew very real.

Panic threatened to take over despite all her efforts. Where was she? Who were they? And what did they intend to do with her?

"Listen to me, little lady," the voice ordered gently but gravely. "It's important that you be quiet for a few minutes." Curiously, she'd have sworn there was concern in the words.

This didn't make sense, she thought, a part of her mind functioning under the nearly all-pervading fear. The voice and the hands were gentle. But what gentle man would kidnap a woman in the middle of the night, bind, blindfold and gag her and stuff her into the back of a car? The answer was beyond her. Could she be dreaming?

A car door opened and she was tugged backward by the hems of her jeans until an arm could reach around her while another gently pushed her head down so that she didn't bump it. She was tossed over a shoulder and her captor began to walk.

No, she decided as her ribs bumped painfully and her stomach began to roil. This was no dream.

She struggled and made as much noise as she could through the fabric around her mouth.

"Lady, please!" the voice said. "Just be quiet another minute."

Perversely, she wriggled and tried to kick, making unintelligible noises behind the gag.

"God!" The second voice spoke at last. It was raspy and soft. "You sure we done the right thing?"

"Yeah . . . sure," the first voice replied. "Sure." To Kellen's ear, he didn't sound convinced.

The right thing?

She heard a heavy door close, then the shoulder over which she lay suspended, rose and fell with a deep sigh.

The second voice muttered a quiet but heartfelt profanity. "We made it."

Made it? Made it where? Why did they sound as though they were in danger also?

Now confused as well as frightened, not to mention extremely uncomfortable, Kellen lay still as they seemed to climb stairs.

A door opened, the man carrying her walked a small distance, then tipped her off his shoulder. She screamed behind the gag as she free fell a small distance then landed on something cool and soft. A bed.

"If you promise to be quiet," the first voice told her, helping her to sit up, "I'll take off the gag and untie your hands."

Kellen didn't have to think about it. She nodded vigorously.

The moment the gag was removed, she screamed lustily.

"I told him you can't trust 'em," the first voice said with genuine indignation. "Didn't I tell him you can't trust 'em?"

Another door opened to Kellen's left and a cold ripple of apprehension worked up her spine. She turned her head in that direction, waiting, her lips parted, for whatever would happen next.

The silence in the room was deafening. She could feel the tension even without seeing it. "No." A man's voice spoke the word softly and flatly.

There was another moment's silence, then the man's voice repeated, louder and laced with grim reluctance. "Oh, no. My God. Gordy, tell me you didn't *do* this!"

Kellen felt the mattress take another weight. Her hands still tied behind her back she tottered unsteadily then fell over and was caught in a pair of arms. Her cheek collided with something solid.

"Damn it, Gordy." Fingers worked at the knot on her blindfold. "Spike, what in the hell is wrong with you guys?"

Judging by the voice above her head, Kellen guessed that her cheek rested against a shoulder. She inhaled a dark, musky fragrance and felt the gentle grate of beard against her temple. Fingers cupped the nape of her neck and pulled her head up. Strong hands steadied her, then the blindfold was yanked from her eyes and tossed aside.

She looked into the distressed eyes of the prince. As she stared at him, mouth agape, his eyes went over her feature by feature. In confusion she tried to speak, couldn't find her voice, cleared her throat and tried again.

"I don't understand," she croaked, fear leaving her with only a whisper of a voice.

He closed his eyes, ran a hand over his face and shook his head. "No, I'm sure you don't." He reached around her to untie her hands.

"Boss, you said..." A short, broad man came forward into the pool of light near the bed. Kellen recognized him as one of the two men who were always with the prince. A glance into the shadows revealed the second one. "'It would make the whole thing more bearable,'" he seemed to be quoting, "'to have the green-eyed angel from the window in my bed.' That's what you said, boss."

The prince exploded to his feet. He wore jeans, Kellen noted, and a simple black sweater with a leather shooting patch on the shoulder.

"I didn't mean it, Gordy!" he roared at the shorter man, who squared his shoulders and took it. "I was just talking! I didn't expect you to *kidnap* her!"

Gordy adjusted his jacket in the sudden quiet that followed the prince's shout.

"Rocco said we're supposed to keep you happy," he argued reasonably. "Get you everything you want."

The second man came out of the shadows to stand beside his companion. "We was doing our jobs, boss. That's all. No need to yell at Gordy."

With a groan, the prince turned away from the two men and ran a hand down his face again.

He really was gorgeous, Kellen thought. As gorgeous in a temper as he was when he smiled. But she was a little surprised that he had no European accent. His speech pattern was very all-American.

And apparently this had all been a mistake. She felt a little giddy with relief and the proximity of the prince.

He turned back to the two men and said in a quieter but thoroughly exasperated tone, "Didn't it occur to you that you would scare her to death? That we're trying to lay low and you've done something that'll have every law enforcement agency in four counties looking for you?"

So he was a criminal. Kellen absorbed that information with surprise superseding fear. That was a possibility she hadn't considered. He looked too...handsome to be hiding anything ugly. Ugliness had to show somewhere.

Gordy and Spike exchanged an uncomfortable glance.

"Did you break into her home?" the prince demanded quietly.

"Oh, no, boss," Gordy replied righteously, looking offended at the suggestion. "We took her off the street when she finished doing the window at the shoe store."

"You might have been seen."

"No," Gordy denied emphatically. "We was careful."

"Where's her vehicle?"

"What?"

"Her vehicle. The red van that was in front of that dress shop yesterday while she was working."

"Well, we left it . . . I mean we didn't . . ."

The door from the hallway burst open and a tall, slender gray-haired man with a buzz cut stood on the threshhold. His eyes widened with horror when they fell on Kellen.

"Who's that?" he asked tightly.

The prince spared a condemning glance for his men before replying calmly, "A young lady from town."

The man took several steps into the room, his expression one of disbelief. "You didn't send for a . . ."

The prince rolled his eyes. "No, I didn't. I saw her a few nights ago when Gordy and Spike and I were walking. I expressed a certain . . ." his glance bounced off Kellen, both appreciative and apologetic ". . . interest in her and they took me literally. They brought her to me."

"That's it!" the man shouted, stepping aside to point to the door. "Those two amoeba brains are out of here!"

"No, they're not," the prince corrected quietly.

"Look!" The man walked to within several inches of the prince. Gordy and Spike held their ground. Kellen thought with mild hysteria that they looked like a quarrel on a baseball field. "*I'm* running your life until this is over."

The prince held his angry gaze, his own icily calm. "No one runs my life but me. They're my friends. They're staying."

The man's resolve seem to waver just a little. "They're going to get you killed, Dom. If we don't do things my way, I can't guarantee your safety. This was supposed to be a safe hiding place. First, you insist on going out at night. You alone might have been one thing, but the three of you together may as well have a brass band."

"You ain't seen any holes in him, have you, Burton?" Gordy asked, getting in the other man's face. "We was sent here by his uncle to take care of him, and if he wants to take walks, we'll see that he takes walks and that nothing happens to him when he does."

The gray-haired man pushed him aside with a strength that apparently startled Gordy.

"Now they bring you a woman." He continued his conversation with the prince as though nothing had disturbed it. "What are we going to do with a broad if Mueller finds you? You know she can't leave."

"What do you mean I can't leave?" Kellen pushed herself off the bed, galvanized into action. Seeing the prince again was one thing, but being mistaken for a prostitute quite another. "Watch this."

She turned toward the door, intent on walking through it and down the stairs and out into the night, whoever or whatever Mueller was. Gorgeous prince or not, this was simply too confusing.

A long arm reached out to catch her and draw her back. The prince's grip was gentle but impossible to escape. As she pulled against him, he brought her securely to his side.

He frowned at Burton. "What do you mean, she can't leave?"

"She knows where you are," Burton stated as though it should be obvious.

"No, I don't." Kellen's voice came out high and anxious. "They blindfolded me. I have no idea *where* I am. And even if I did, I don't know who *he* is." She indicated the prince with a gesture of her free hand. "So that would make it impossible for me to tell anyone *where* he is."

Burton shook his head, apparently unimpressed with her incoherent argument. "No one leaves here. That's a rule I won't budge from until this is over."

"Burton . . ." the prince began reasonably.

"Dom, even if you're willing to compromise your own safety, think about your boys. Any loose ends that can lead back to you can also lead back to them. She stays."

Kellen looked up at the prince, waiting for him to offer another argument on her behalf. Instead, he ran a hand down his face and turned her toward the side door through which he'd come.

"Excuse us," he said to the three men. "I have to explain things to . . . what's your name?"

"It doesn't matter," she said with a firmness that hid a redeveloping fear. "We aren't going to know each other that long. Mr. Burton may be the final word to you, but he isn't to me."

She tried for the other door but the prince caught her again just as Burton blocked the opening with his body. Almost more like an embrace than capture, the prince pinned both of her arms around her and held her back against his chest.

"That isn't going to work," he said quietly. "What we have to do is talk about this. Now, what's your name?"

She considered refusing to tell him, then accepted that she could not fight four men for her freedom. She sighed. "Kellen Clark."

"Kellen." He repeated the name, looking down into her eyes. "It's like you, small but mysterious."

She raised an eyebrow. "Mysterious? I'm not the one who wanders around at night dressed in black, with bodyguards who kidnap people and won't let them go."

"No," he said. "You just show up in a store window as though some magician breathed life into a beautiful mannequin with eyes the color of a Christmas tree."

She stared at him, startled by the extravagance of the compliment.

He looked away from her to Gordy. "You'd better make sure we're secure. And get her van in our garage."

"Right, boss."

"Great!" the white-haired man raved as he followed the two bodyguards from the room. "Now I have to deal with a temperamental writer, two mob thugs, and a stubborn broad."

"I keep telling you," Gordy protested. "Rocco's not with the mob."

Kellen heard the other man's voice raise in volume as he continued. "I don't get paid enough for this! I'm going to call..."

The prince closed the door to the adjoining room, cutting off the sound.

Kellen found herself in what appeared to be a makeshift office with all the comforts of a sitting room.

A portable electric typewriter sat on a folding metal table, a kitchen chair pulled up to it. On a card table beside it stood a telephone, a fat Rolodex, a tape recorder, and open books and scribbled notes on every inch of free surface.

The room was bisected by a brown leather sofa. On one wall was a small kitchen with running water. A brick fireplace with a cheerful fire made up one wall. The other was curtained.

He took her coat from her, placed it over the back of a chair, then gestured her to the sofa. He went to one of the cupboards above the length of tiled counter and removed a short squat bottle and two snifters.

"I don't want anything to drink," she said with cool firmness. Curiosity, she told herself, was the only thing making her amenable. She wanted to know what was going on, then she wanted out of here.

She was further unsettled by the sight of a pistol tucked into his belt, nestled against the small of his broad back. It looked both lethal and out of place in the cozy room.

He smiled at her over his shoulder and poured the rich amber liquid into both glasses.

"You might change your mind when I explain the situation." He brought the snifters to the sofa and placed one on the low glass coffee table. The other he rolled back and forth in long, supple fingers as he sat beside her.

Kellen watched him with a strange sense of unreality. It was almost as though she was watching this scene unfold from behind one of the many store windows that were her livelihood. This could not actually be happening to her.

She forced a deep tone of voice and a square set to her chin. "It had better be good."

As he continued to roll the snifter slowly in his hands, he looked into her eyes and she got the feeling he saw right through her attempt to sound tough to the concern and confusion inside her.

"Oh, it's very good." His voice was wry as he handed her the brandy, then picked up the other.

Her glass was warm from his hands and spilled a little in her own as her fingers shook. She knew the flavor of the brandy would be heightened by the heat. She felt curiously reluctant to put it to her lips.

"My name is Dominic Hunter," he began, then hesitated as though awaiting a reaction. When she waited for him to go on, he asked with an accepting grin, "Doesn't mean anything to you?"

"From now on it will mean a lot to me," she said judiciously, her tone suggesting that none of it would be positive. "If you mean do I recognize it..." Something jangled faintly in her memory, but she had no idea why. She allowed herself the indulgence of administering a snub while realizing she was finally going to find out what she'd been wondering for days.

"I don't. Are you a rock star? A politician? A junk-bond king evading the law?"

He acknowledged the jab with a broadening of his grin. "I'm a writer. You used one of my books in your display when you did the bookstore window."

A writer. That was a possibility she hadn't considered. "Was your book so bad that you need protection?"

"Kellen, you have a mean streak," he scolded, still grinning. "Actually, I've topped the bestseller list four times running. I write true crime."

"True crime..." she repeated. "You mean...real mysteries?"

He sipped at the brandy, then propped a foot on the glass coffee table and rested the snifter on his knee.

"Real *crime*. Books about front-page news. The person I write about has always been convicted, but I do extensive research to inform the reader of how and why the criminal did what he did. Or she. You have one of the finest craftsmen of the genre right here in the northwest—Ann Rule."

She nodded. That was a familiar name. But she'd always thought interest in the details of grisly murders ghoulish.

"I like Erma Bombeck, myself," she told him. "Life can be grim enough. How can you sleep nights knowing what went on in the murderer's brain? Or don't you? Maybe that's why you wander around at night like some exiled prince."

An elegant dark eyebrow rose at her concept of him. She wished the words back too late.

"Exiled prince?" he asked, putting his glass on the table and turning to lean an elbow on the back of the sofa and study her with interest.

She stared into her brandy then sipped it, desperately needing something to do to avoid his eyes.

"I've seen you walking down the street every night this week—always after midnight, always dressed in black, always accompanied by bodyguards." She shrugged and swirled the brandy in her glass so vigorously she half expected the small vortex to draw her in. "I guess my imagination filled in what my intelligence couldn't know."

"I like that." His voice quieted, spilled over her, warm and thick and mellow. "On so few facts, you turned me into a prince. Why not a thief or a stalker?"

She smiled thinly. "I did consider that you might be a vampire, but I dismissed the thought when I remembered that Dracula never traveled with bodyguards."

Dominic couldn't believe she was sitting here beside him—the angel from the clothing-store window—who seemed to have wit and intelligence as well as beauty. She'd been dropped into the debilitating tedium of his confinement like a gift from God to keep him going.

He smiled as he pondered the thought. Actually she'd been dropped in by Gordy and Spike who were on orders to cater to his every whim. He couldn't help but be grateful he'd expressed that one aloud.

Until he remembered that being here placed her in the same danger in which he found himself. But letting her go might very possibly be worse. Despite Burton protecting him, and the two seasoned if quirky hoods his uncle had sent, *he* felt responsible for her safety. And he would let nothing endanger his boys. That meant she had to spend the next few days at his side.

He drew a deep breath as he prepared to break it to her.

"Are you hiding out because of your connection with the mob?" she asked, forestalling him.

She was a pretty thing, he thought, looking into her questioning green eyes. She had porcelain skin, a light smattering of freckles over a very regal, gracefully pointed Candice Bergen nose, and thick, shoulder-length maple brown hair he could hardly keep his hands from touching.

"My uncle's not with the mob. He has his own operation going. He's my mother's brother. He's always kept a safe distance from us, unless we needed help or money, then he always found out about it, and he always provided." He shrugged with acceptance. "He meant well when he sent Gordy and Spike. He doesn't trust someone who isn't connected with family to do the job."

"Why are you hiding?"

He stood up to stretch his legs. A part of him still couldn't help but wish he wrote men's adventure and could make things up out of his imagination.

He went to the drapes, intending to open them as he'd done contrary to orders every night this week, then remembered he now had Kellen's safety to consider as well as his own. Instead, he turned away and paced the width of the room.

Kellen watched him move and couldn't dispel the prince image. He had the presence. And with his hair a little too long, the leather patch on the shoulder of his sweater that might have been an epaulet, and the long, graceful stride that made her see a sword scabbard slapping against his lean jean-clad thigh, he could have been the dream come true of some medieval maiden.

It was fortunate that she herself was very twentieth-century.

He picked up a poker and stirred the fire. "Does the name Jason Morley ring a bell even if my name didn't?" he asked.

It did. Several months ago, his trial had saturated the news.

"Of course," she replied. "He killed that entrepreneur in New York."

"Massachusetts," Dominic corrected. "Warren Bowles. And Morley didn't do it."

"But he was found guilty. He's on death row."

"I know. But he didn't do it. In my research, I stumbled upon the real killer."

"Who is it?"

"Another businessman, an associate of Bowles in a few dubious land deals. A guy named Mueller. Bowles tried to pull out of their partnership and Mueller, afraid he'd talk about this shady business, killed him."

"But the *Globe* said Morley had been sleeping with Bowles's wife. That he was worth millions."

Dominic nodded. "Convincing motive, but that's not what happened."

"How do you know?"

He smiled ruefully. "Because Mrs. Bowles told me the truth."

Kellen frowned as she waited for him to continue.

"She was at a charity function that night, but she'd come home early with a headache. She saw the whole thing. She was so terrified of what Mueller would do to her if he knew she was a witness that she let everyone believe she'd gone for a long walk to clear her head and didn't get home until well after the murder."

Kellen tried to assimilate all the implications. "But she's letting her lover take the wrap."

"She told me the truth one night at an Art League party. She'd had too much champagne, I walked her out onto the patio for some fresh air, and she told me what really happened."

"So, she's going to straighten it all out."

He took a long sip of his brandy. "I don't know. I went to her place the next morning to record her story and try to convince her to go to the district attorney, but apparently her hangover brought second thoughts because she had packed her bags and left."

"Did you call the police?"

He shook his head. "Interesting problem there. Remember the shady connections I mentioned? When Mrs. Bowles told me about Mueller, I looked into his corporation and found it'd been making monthly payments to a foreign account held by guess who?"

She took a wild guess. "The police chief?"

"Close. The commissioner."

"No!"

"Instead of calling the police, I called my uncle, asking him to lend me some of his connections to find Mrs. Bowles. But the very next day, Mueller sent someone after me. Rocco decided to hide me and my family until he can find Bowles's widow and make her go to the district attorney."

She was beginning to understand. She saw it in the dark gaze fixed on her from across the room. "Mueller's trying to kill you."

"Yes."

"Well." She digested that grisly news, then tried to put it out of her mind. This was just too bizarre for a window dresser from Sandpiper. She sighed and took another sip of brandy. Then she stood. "I sympathize," she said, wandering toward the bedroom, intent on finding her way out. "I really do. But you have lots of protection here, and there really isn't anything I can do."

She felt color fill her cheeks as she recalled what had prompted his uncle's men to kidnap her. She cleared her throat and tugged at the lapels of her denim jacket. "I'm flattered by your fantasy, but I'm not really looking for a man. So, if you don't mind, I have a big day tomorrow. I have to..."

His height and formidable shoulders blocked the doorway. His smile was reluctant and apologetic. "Kellen, I can't let you go."

"Dominic," she stated gravely, firming her stance, "if you don't step out of my way this instant, I will use my extensive knowledge of Tai Kwan Do on you and you won't have to worry about this Mueller person any longer."

The threat was too loaded with interesting possibilities to ignore.

He rested his hands on his hips in an attitude of waiting. "Do your best," he said solemnly.

She lunged at him without hesitation, the movement accompanied by a high, ominous cry. Afraid a block on his part would hurt her, he simply stood still, prepared to endure the blow. His strategy was both chivalrous and duplicitous. While it would prevent her from being bruised, it would also undoubtedly end in body contact, a thought he'd been considering since the moment he found her bound and blindfolded in the middle of his bed.

But her stiffly poised hand stopped an inch from his throat, and closer observation revealed that her stance was more balletic than lethal.

They stared at each other for a moment, he longing to close the mere inch between them, she horrified that he hadn't even flinched.

"Was that it?" he asked finally.

She lowered her hand and folded her arms.

"Yeah." She leaned against the doorway, her glance up at him self-deprecating as she shuffled a foot. "I lied about the extensive knowledge."

"Well, I was impressed," he said consolingly. "But if you ever try it on someone else, try not to look so much like a swan while you're doing it. And your hand should connect with something vulnerable. A windpipe or the bridge of a nose."

"A swan?" she asked softly.

He brushed the hair back from her face. "Yes. You looked like Odile in *Swan Lake*. You could get creamed that way."

"Look," she reasoned, shaking off his touch. It seemed to be pulling her places she didn't want to go. The prince and a swan... "It's illegal for you to keep me here against my will."

Green eyes flashed at him, and he guessed there was a stubborn woman within the swan. Teasing her had been an intriguing diversion, but it was time to put the situation in terms she could not mistake.

"Is it your will to get your pretty head blown off?" he asked.

Kellen straightened at the question, half indignant, half afraid. He appeared very serious. She didn't imagine he was the type of man who indulged in dramatics. His business was facts. Looking into his eyes she lost all indignation. She was now one-hundred percent afraid.

"If you remember the news story," he said, "the killer also got Bowles's housekeeper, a sweet little old lady with a bad leg. Shot her in the head. Do you imagine he'd think twice about you?"

She looked over her shoulder as though expecting Mueller to appear. "He's . . . here?"

"Not yet. But he found me in Connecticut when it got back to him that I was investigating and sent someone after me. He must have been watching Bowles's house, saw me go there and by nature of what I do probably figured out what I was up to."

"Then, how did Mrs. Bowles get away?"

"That I don't know."

"Why isn't *your* head blown off?" she asked coolly, attempting to show him his choice of words had neither shocked her, nor frightened her. Which wasn't true, but the need to appear in control of her destiny when he was trying to wrest it from her seemed important.

Absently, he put an arm around her shoulders and drew her into the bedroom. "Because I *do* have an extensive knowledge of self-defense, though I prefer good old boxing to the martial arts. I knocked him unconscious."

She looked skeptical. And it helped her pretend nonchalance at finding herself in the bedroom again.

"Then, why isn't he in custody?"

He went to the wide walnut dresser across the room and pulled a drawer open. "Because I had my two sons with me at the time, and four of their friends. We'd just come back from pizza and were getting ready to settle down to a Friday the Thirteenth marathon for my older son's birthday. By the time I locked the kids in the house and got back out, he was gone. My uncle moved me here."

"What does Rocco do, exactly?"

He shook his head. "I'm not sure. I don't think it's anything big, because the mob would never let him operate. Whatever it is, it doesn't interfere with them because they coexist. He once swore to me that he never hurts anybody. Beyond that, we both believe the less I know, the better."

He yanked a burgundy and dark blue paisley something out of the drawer and came toward her with it.

"You should be comfortable in this. I'd give you the bottoms, but..." his eyes slid down to her hips in bold appreciation "...then, what would I have to wear?"

She tossed the pajama top on the bed, fighting fear, frustration, and the smallest twinge of excitement.

"You don't seem to understand that I have a life!" she asserted with a broad thrust of her right hand. "I have things to do. If I don't show up, people will miss me and wonder where I am. That won't be good for you when someone remembers Gordy and Spike's car and traces them here.''

He shook his head, unmoved. "That can't be helped. My uncle's boys aren't always very bright, but they are used to working in the dark. I doubt that anyone saw them. But if they did, we'll deal with it when the time comes.''

Then, as though the question had just occurred to him, he asked quietly, "Are you married?''

"Yes," she lied with an annoyed glower because it was becoming increasingly obvious to her that she was losing this confrontation. "To a bad-tempered front lineman for Notre Dame.''

He shook his head scoldingly. "Come now. We can't be bound together in a life-and-death struggle and lie to each other.''

She thought about her mother, who was writing and partying in Tahoe and might not even call her again for several days. But what if she did and couldn't find her? She'd call Mrs. Watson who lived next door, then Joanie Bigby with whom Kellen spent a lot of her free time. When they reported that they hadn't seen or heard from her, her mother would be frantic.

"I *do* have a mother," she said.

He nodded, understanding her concern. "I'm sorry. But I'm sure she'd be more upset if she lost you permanently, than just for a few days. Is she in Sandpiper?''

Kellen sank onto the edge of the bed, confused, upset. Was this real? She and the prince locked in a house, waiting for a killer? Surely her mind had simply woven the half-remembered plot of an old book around her dreams of the dark mystery man.

He sat beside her. His arm against hers was hard and warm and very, very real.

Accepting that this was indeed happening, she sighed and answered. "She lives in L.A. But she's in Lake Tahoe for a few days."

"Are you in touch every day?"

"No. She just called this afternoon."

"Then this could be over," he said bracingly, "before she even misses you."

"Over?" she questioned in a small voice. It sounded as though termination of this situation could take several unsavory forms.

"You'll be safe." He didn't promise or swear, but the truth of it was there in his eyes. Then he smiled. "You're protected by the Manhattan Security Company, and me. When Mueller shows up, they'll get him, then you and I will be free to have a quiet drink somewhere and figure out whether to pursue this at your place or mine."

She pretended to have no idea what he was talking about. "This?"

"This," he repeated and tilted and lowered his head to take her lips.

She put a hand to his chest and held him away. "You have children."

His eyes roved her features. "Yes, I do."

"That usually requires a mother."

"It did." His wandering gaze stopped at her eyes, and she saw a flash of sadness in his. "She passed away two years ago."

Kellen frowned in surprise, the hand that held him away slackening.

He closed the small space between them and kissed her.

He tasted as dark and velvet as he looked, she thought, fascination blocking any notion she'd had of resisting. His kiss was tender and warm like a summer shadow, long and sweet and mystifying.

Dominic felt the sparkle of her on his lips, as though he'd tasted a snowflake, or a star. She was like a balm to the lonely longing of the last two years, this animated angel from the Christmas window.

He raised his head, thinking this was not the moment to complicate things further. But there would come a time. She looked wide-eyed and startled.

"You take a lot for granted," she whispered.

He smiled without apology. "It's the way I am." Then he stood and pointed to an open door in a corner of the room.

"Bathroom's in there. Bath, shower, Jacuzzi, even a clean toothbrush in the bottom of the cabinet." Then he pointed back toward the office. "I'll be in there. If you need anything, just holler."

"Don't you sleep?" she asked.

He shook his head. "I've been working most of the night since I've been here."

"Where are your boys?" she asked.

A smile filled with love and concern came and went. "In protective custody at another location."

She sighed, thinking how complicated life had suddenly become. "I'm sorry about your wife, Dominic."

The brief pain of the memory, he thought, was worth the sound of his name on her lips.

"I'm adjusted. We had a wonderful marriage, and a lot of her is still with me. But life goes on. Get some sleep." He stepped into the office and closed the door behind him.

Kellen rubbed the tingle of his kiss from her lips and tried to banish that glimpse of his sadness from her memory. She ran the shower so he would think she was falling in with his plans, then hid the pajama top in the hamper. With the water running, she tiptoed to the drapes that matched the ones in the office, and peeked between them. Just as she thought. French windows.

After a few moments she turned off the shower and climbed into bed fully dressed, pulling the blankets up to her chin. She was surrounded by the combined scents of fabric softener and the dark headiness of his cologne. She closed her eyes and turned her mind off to all the thoughts that tried to plague her, and the sharp memory of the kiss.

She had to pull her wits together if she was going to escape when all was quiet.

Dominic was gorgeous and definitely intriguing, but the situation was simply too bizarre to fit into her agenda. She felt a desperate need to get out of it. Not only because of physical danger, though that was certainly considerable; but because she sensed another danger here she wasn't equipped to handle.

IN THE OFFICE, Dominic stared at the two words on the otherwise blank page in the typewriter. "Chapter Six." The Smith Corona hummed and waited, demanding brilliant prose.

He didn't have a thought in his head that didn't involve the little brunette in the next room. As though he wasn't in enough trouble.

THE HOUSE WAS SILENT in less than an hour. Kellen heard the asthmatic rumble of her van going into the garage, the exchange of conversation downstairs. A door closed, then another, and she guessed that two of the three men had gone to bed, leaving the third on guard. But he'd be watching for invasion, not escape.

From the office came the faint click of typewriter keys.

Kellen inched quietly out of bed in the darkness. She slipped her hand between the drapes and found ice-cold glass and the lock on the latch.

She flicked it, wincing against the loud "snick" in the quiet room. The door rumbled softly on its track.

She stepped out into the cold darkness of a veranda, thinking belatedly about her coat and deciding to leave it. Her good fortune continued when she spotted the almost bare mountain ash tree just beyond the railing. She extended a hand to it and found it just beyond her reach. No matter. A well-aimed leap executed with confidence and she'd be on her way home.

A nagging little sense of loss surfaced, but she pushed it down. Dominic Hunter was out of her life starting now.

DOMINIC WASN'T SURE why he heard the noise. It had been barely audible—the faintest rustle of fabric. A small sound of the wind.

His work had conditioned him. The best clues were whispered exchanges or conversations that were overheard. Or it might have been because he'd been a father so long. His ear was always cocked for a sound that suggested rash, inexperienced and potentially dangerous behavior.

He was out of his chair and in the bedroom in an instant. He hesitated the space of a heartbeat, saw the open doors and Kellen astride the patio railing, reaching for a branch of the tree still a hand span away.

His heart in his throat, he took two strides over the bed and caught her arm just as she overbalanced and fell sideways with a little scream.

Kellen felt as though her arm was being ripped off when the shadowy garden rising up to meet her abruptly stopped. A hand caught the belt of her jeans and yanked her up to the railing, then unceremoniously hooked an arm under her leg and lifted her over, onto the veranda. A shove pushed her into the bedroom.

The overhead light glared on as Burton raced into the room, gun drawn.

"It's all right," Dominic said quietly, closing and locking the doors then drawing the drapes.

"What happened?" Burton demanded.

Gordy appeared behind him in a pair of loud striped pajamas, an Uzi in one hand, Spike beside him in his underwear, pointing a handgun.

"I tried to escape," Kellen gasped crossly as she started to rebutton the blouse that had come undone when Dominic had grabbed her. She was surprised to discover that she still had her left arm. It ached abominably but it was still attached.

Her buttons, however, were not. She crossed the fabric tightly around her. "Are you really surprised?"

Burton returned his gun to its shoulder holster. Gordy leaned in relief against the door frame as Spike relaxed his stance.

Burton's frustrated gaze went from Dominic to Kellen, then back to Dominic again. "Make her understand," he commanded, "before we're all dead, that she's not leaving here." He slammed out of the room.

Gordy and Spike shared a guilty look, then followed.

Dominic, expression like granite, looked around the room. "Where's the pajama top?"

She glared at him. "I threw it in the hamper."

He went to the dresser, withdrew a long-sleeved white T-shirt, and handed it to her. She pulled it over her head, yanked the ruined shirt out from under it, and balled it angrily in her hands.

Feeling foolish, embarrassed, and just a little frightened after her near-plunge two stories, she looked at Dominic with deliberate defiance.

"You can't make me stay," she told him.

He took her arm no more gently than he had when he saved her from tumbling over the railing and marched her into the office. He closed the door behind them, pulled her to the leather sofa and pushed her onto it. He sat beside her and pinned her with a dark, calm gaze.

"I'm a nice guy," he said reasonably, "when things go my way. When they don't, somebody usually pays." He paused a moment to let that sink in.

It crossed Kellen's mind that he was acting—that this was a tough-guy routine intended to frighten her into cooperation. But his eyes were just dark enough and steady enough that she couldn't be sure.

"I have every intention of seeing my kids again," he went on quietly. "And I'm not going to allow you to prevent that. I know this isn't your fault—"

"It's yours," she interupted, folding her arms so he wouldn't see her tremble. "This is your fault."

"Then trust me to make it right. And do as I say."

"I want to go home," she insisted.

"So do I," he agreed. "Preferably alive." Then without warning he stood, took hold of her ankles and swung them up onto the sofa.

He left for a moment and came back with a pillow and blanket. She raised her head so that he could place the pillow, then ignored him as he spread the blanket over her.

"From now on," he told her, "you stay with me. It'll be easier on both of us if you don't fight it."

She punched the pillow. "You don't know much about today's woman, do you?"

He tucked the blanket in at her shoulder. "You'll be pleasantly surprised to learn that I do," he said, a smile in his voice, "when I have time to show you." He patted her back. "Good night."

Exhausted and resigned to her fate, at least temporarily, Kellen drifted off to the click and hum of the typewriter.

She stirred a level below wakefulness hours later when arms lifted her off the sofa. She struggled, remembering vaguely a conversation about danger, a midair slip.

"Whoa," Dominic's voice said gently. "It's all right. I'm just taking you to bed."

It occurred to her drowsy brain that that was simply danger of another kind, but she was settled against a sturdy shoulder and held close as a blanket was drawn over her. She fell asleep again, concern overpowered by comfort.

Chapter Three

Three strong raps sounded on the bedroom door, followed by the sound of Gordy's voice. "Breakfast, little lady."

Kellen, tucking the slack of bedspread under the pillows, straightened, marched to the door and yanked it open.

"My name is—" She was momentarily rendered mute by the sight of the short, thick man in a blue and white bistro apron. Under it was a white shirt and tie. Below it were neatly creased dark pants and shiny wing tips.

He was smiling, apologetically, she thought.

He held up a tray covered with a towel. "Breakfast," he said.

She took it from him, determined that if she had to stay here, she would establish her position.

"My name is Kellen," she said politely. "Please don't call me 'little lady.'"

"Ellen?" he asked.

"Kellen," she repeated, emphasizing the K as she took the tray from him.

He frowned. "Weird name for a pretty little…" He stopped himself as she squared her shoulders. "Uh, unusual name for a pretty young lady." The elegant rephrasing was delivered in broad Runyonesque.

"I'm named after my parents," she explained defensively, "Kelly and Mary Ellen. Kellen."

He nodded, but didn't appear to understand or approve. He looked over her shoulder into the room. "Where's the boss?"

"I have no idea," she replied. She had awakened alone in the bed without her jeans, vaguely haunted by memories of being held and soothed. Inside, she was a mass of conflicting concerns. She felt the excitement of the brink of some important discovery, and the trepidation of learning more than she wanted to know. And right beside that was the frightening knowledge that she was confined with a man who was being pursued by a killer.

"Isn't he in the office?" Gordy asked anxiously.

"I don't think so." Judging by the quiet beyond the door, she'd guessed he was downstairs.

"Well, he isn't in the kitchen or the living room," Gordy said, his gaze sharpening. With that he pushed past her, lumbered across the bedroom and threw open the office door.

THE THIN LINE of concentration Dominic had scraped together about an hour earlier erupted and vanished as the office door burst open. He swung up and around to confront the intruder, adrenaline pumping.

"Boss!" Gordy shouted.

"What?" he demanded, already running toward the bedroom. Could something have happened he hadn't heard? Could Kellen have been in danger without—?

"Are you okay?" Gordy shouted, catching him by the arms. Dominic began to push him off, then noticed Kellen standing in the middle of the room, apparently in perfect health, holding a tray.

He frowned down at Gordy. "Of course, I'm okay. Why?"

Gordy, obviously feeling foolish, pointed at Kellen. "Well, she didn't know where you was."

"Where am I usually?" Dominic demanded. "In the office working." He was short-tempered because he'd spent the longest few hours of his life with Kellen curled against him. He'd finally had to get up and take a shower or do himself severe mental and bodily harm.

"Well," Gordy replied, voice rising in agitation. "I thought you was gonna be with her. When she hadn't seen you, I thought you was in trouble."

Dominic opened his mouth to deliver a heated reply, but was halted by the genuine concern in the man's eyes. According to the guidelines Uncle Rocco had set down, Gordy was only doing his job.

He placed a hand on the man's shoulder. "Well, I'm fine." He steered him firmly to the door to the hallway. "You can relax."

"I'm sorry, boss. I thought . . ."

Dominic pushed him gently through the doorway. "It's okay, Gordy. I appreciate your vigilance. When this is over I'll be sure Rocco knows what a good job you've done."

Dominic closed the door as Gordy strutted away.

Kellen sat on the edge of the bed with her tray, forcing herself to look Dominic in the eye as he came toward her. She had a fuzzy memory of snuggling in his arms last night. That made indignation seem out of place this morning. And she refused to be embarrassed.

"Don't let Gordy get to you," he advised, sitting on the other side of the tray. "Believe me that I never expected this to happen. And now that it has, I'd never assume that my personal fantasies were also yours."

She eyed him steadily. "I woke up without my jeans."

"Because you were pulling at them in your sleep. I took them off." He grinned. "Tempting as it was to go further, I didn't think I'd be able to convince a jury that your three inches of panties were also making you uncomfortable."

"Funny."

She whipped the towel off the tray, prepared to fortify herself with a hearty breakfast, and stared. It was a hotdog slathered with brown mustard, and waffle-cut french fries.

She uttered a startled little gasp.

Dominic sat up for a closer look.

"Sorry. I should have warned you. My bodyguards are not known for their culinary talents."

She reached longingly for the coffee cup, able to tell before she'd lifted it within a foot of her nose that it was the kind that could eat a spoon. Fortunately, since she worked most nights, it was the kind of coffee she was used to. It kept her awake.

She took a sip and reacted with a delicate shudder and a not very delicate, "Ugh!" It tasted like nuclear waste dripped through a filter. Disappointed and hungry and desperately needing a boost of caffeine, she put the cup down and stared disconsolately at the hot dog.

"I don't suppose you'd prefer a cheese and broccoli omelette?" Dominic asked. "And freshly ground French roast coffee?"

"Don't tease me," she warned, replacing the towel over the tray.

"I'm sure I won't be able to help myself." He stood and pulled her up beside him. "But right now, I'm serious." He retained her hand as he left the bedroom and started down a winding oak staircase.

It was a fairly large and elegant house, she noted, as she hurried to keep up with him. She kept her eyes studiously away from the gun tucked into his back again this morning.

She saw light wood moldings, subdued overstuffed furniture and nautical appointments. Spike watched television from a big chair while Burton sat in a corner of the sofa with his breakfast hot dog. All the drapes were drawn as though it was still night. A measure against Mueller, she guessed.

Spike gave Kellen a cautious smile. Burton watched her pass with vague suspicion and complete disapproval.

The kitchen featured a modern skylight that allowed the glaring brightness of an overcast day to shine off sand-colored counters and appliances. Forest green trims and towels and seat cushions on the farmstead chairs around the small oak table lent the room a cozy atmosphere.

"Where's Gordy?" she asked. "Did I hurt his feelings about breakfast?"

"It's his watch," Dominic explained, opening the refrigerator door and pointing her to the table. "He's out there somewhere. Have a seat. Want some tomato juice?"

"You have something that healthy?" She ignored the kitchen chairs and wandered around the spacious L-shaped room instead to study a shelf of cookbooks.

"Yeah," he replied, squatting down to reach something in the back. "We use it for Bloody Marys."

He emerged from the refrigerator, his arms filled with eggs, a plastic produce bag, a block of cheese, a cube of butter and a pot of jam. He set it all on the counter, then reached back into the refrigerator for the bottle of tomato juice and poured two glasses.

"Does Burton work for your uncle?" Kellen studied a shelf of decorative tins.

"No, my agent hired him, but my uncle had already sent Gordy and Spike. Neither of them will leave the job to the other so I have three bodyguards." Dominic sipped his juice, then placed the broccoli in a colander under running water while he whipped eggs in a bowl. He paused to hand Kellen the block of cheese. "There's a grater in the drawer where you're standing, and a pullout cutting board right above it. This is Burton's aunt's house. She's somewhere in the Bahamas right now."

She looked at Dominic from across the room, arms folded. "I like to think of myself as a guest," she declared. "Why should *I* grate the cheese?"

He glanced at her with a grin. "It'll be ready to eat sooner."

That, she thought, wandering toward the counter, was a good argument.

He put butter into a pan, turned the burner on low, then turned off the faucet and patted the broccoli dry.

"Burton and your uncle's men don't seem to get along very well," Kellen observed.

"Understatement. They're engaged in a constant power struggle." He held up several stalks of green onion. "How do you feel about onions sautéed with the broccoli?"

She made an appreciative sound as a little mound of shredded cheese began to form under the grater. "I'd love it."

He washed them off, then with a practiced sweep of a broad-bladed knife moved her grated cheese to the side of the board.

"It's curious," he said as he chopped. "That you're offended at the thought of hot dogs for breakfast, but you'll eat onions."

"Well, onions are different. They're..." she made an expressive gesture with her hands "...they're like gold jewelry. They go with anything."

"Creative comparison." He scooped the onions onto the edge of the blade and, protecting it with his left hand, carried them to the sizzling butter and dropped them in. "Want to bring the broccoli?"

Kellen made a cup of her hands and dropped the broccoli into the pan. The aroma was already magnificent. She was accustomed to cereal for breakfast.

"Funny," she said, watching him control the contents of the pan with a wooden spatula. "I thought someone who'd made the bestseller list four times running would have a cook."

"I do. She's with my boys."

"But you look as if you know what you're doing."

"I do." He wiped his hands on a handy towel. "I cook for my kids on weekends. Before that..." The little trace of sadness touched his eyes. Then he busied himself with putting bread in the toaster. "Before that, when the boys were small, my wife worked as a legal secretary and I stayed home, trying to launch a writing career. So I did all the cooking."

"What happened?" she asked gently.

"Cancer," he replied. "Sudden and quick. It was over in several months."

So that touching look in his eye had more to do with the rigors of real life than the romantic tales she'd spun from behind her windows.

"I am sorry." She'd told him so before, but now that she understood a little more, felt obliged to say it again.

He made a "that's life" gesture with his hands, then turned his attention back to the fry pan.

"She left me with two great kids and a lot of comforting memories." He dropped the eggs into the pan, then put the bowl aside and turned to Kellen. "I miss them like hell right now."

"How old are they?" She hoped that talking about them might relieve the loneliness.

"Nine and fourteen," he replied, grinning to himself as he added the cheese to the bubbling egg mixture. "Ethan's the oldest. Into football, food, grisly details, and anything mechanical. He's a lot like me, except that you couldn't pay him enough to read a book. Travis is a gentle soul like his mother. Loves animals and nature, and shows surprising capabilities with carpentry."

"No writer gene in him, either?"

He shook his head and expertly folded the omelette. "Not that I can see."

Kellen opened the cupboard above her head and found it filled with fine china. She closed it quickly and tried the next one. It was filled with good, serviceable stoneware. She pulled down plates and cups.

"I guess you'll just have to have a third child," she said chattily, placing the plates beside him. It wasn't until she looked up to ask him where the silverware was that she caught the amused glint in his eye.

"You have a sparkling creative talent," he remarked. "We might very well create a brilliant novelist together."

Her automatic reactions were a blush and a stammer, but she refused to give in to them. Instead, she started opening drawers.

"Really?" she asked, trying to sound preoccupied with her search. "So that's why you had me brought here? An experiment in genetic engineering."

"I didn't have you brought here," he corrected, cutting the omelette in half with the spatula and placing a piece on each plate. "My wishes were misinterpreted." He hesitated, then corrected himself. "No, they weren't misinterpreted, they were implemented when they shouldn't have been." The toast popped. He caught Kellen's wrist and pulled her around him to the other side of the stove.

"Utensils are in there," he said, pointing to the drawer. "Want to hand me a butter knife?"

The warmth of his touch still shackled her wrist as she handed him a knife, handle first. He buttered the toast and carried their plates to the table. "Can you grab the jam?" he asked.

She distributed utensils while he went back to the counter to pour coffee.

Then they were facing each other across the table, and a sudden stirring of electrical awareness spiked the easy congeniality.

"So is that a 'no' on my third child?" he asked, pushing the salt and pepper her way.

"Well, I don't want to be hasty," she replied, avoiding those dark interested eyes while she seasoned her omelette. "But you have to remember that your third child would be *my* first. And you live in Massachusetts..."

"Connecticut," he corrected. "I was researching in Massachusetts. I *live* in Connecticut."

She shrugged off his correction. "Almost the same thing."

He shook his head as though concerned. "Hardly. Our child could be a brilliant novelist as long as he didn't deal with anything geographical."

She reached for the jam. "Not necessarily. My father was a game guide in the Cascades. And my mother writes travel books." She gave him a superior glance as she dolloped thick apricot preserves onto her toast. "So there."

He reached for the jam she pushed his way. "The geography gene must skip a generation."

Kellen speared a bite of omelette and moaned with approval at the crusty outside and the soft cheesy middle with the broccoli perfectly sautéed.

She looked across the table at his grin and knew he expected praise. In all conscience, she couldn't withhold it.

"It's wonderful," she cooed. "I applaud your culinary skill."

"Thank you."

"But on the subject of my poor geography..."

"Yes?"

"It's because I don't want to be anywhere but here." She tore a slice of jammy toast in half and bit off a corner. She chewed and swallowed. "I don't know how anyone who'd ever seen the north coast of Oregon would want to be anywhere else, even posh Connecticut."

"You forget that all I've seen of my surroundings have been in the dark." His gaze rested on her with warm significance. "Except for you."

"The point is," she said, trying to keep the banter light. They were going to spend the next few days only a few feet apart. She had to find some way to keep her distance. "If we had a child together, we'd have to raise it in, say..." She searched her brain to come up with a state that was close to the middle of the country. But except for New England and the west, the rest of the map was a collection of names she knew but couldn't put in their places. She finally gave up. "What state is in the middle?"

"Ah..." He thought. "Kansas, Nebraska, somewhere in there."

She shook her head and pointed her fork definitively. "Well, that does it right there. Plains states. I remember that from school. I *have* to be near the water. I couldn't possibly have a baby in a plains state.

Maternal angst would probably supersede genetic influence and the baby would be born grumpy and wan."

Dominic bit his lip to hold back a grin. He didn't want to give her encouragement. "Grumpy and wan?"

She nodded, chewing, then swallowed. "And very probably allergic to corn and soy and *The Wizard of Oz.*"

"You're missing an important point here."

"What's that?"

"Connecticut's on the water."

His eyes caught hers and held. This was growing serious, she realized. Not about a baby, of course, but about making love. And instinct told her he wasn't driven by the proximity of their circumstances. At least she didn't think he was. But she couldn't imagine that after a three-minute interview through a window, he could be so attracted to Kellen Clark that he would want to make love to her for that reason alone.

Keep it light, she told herself. Because, God help her, she was fighting the same desire visible in his eyes.

She smiled and cut another bite of omelette. "That's eastern water. I need western water."

"Well, maybe with half my genetic makeup the baby would need *eastern* water."

"See?" she said. "It's already getting complicated. Maybe we should just give this a pass until we're more sure of the details." Desperately seeking a way out of the subject, she sipped at her coffee and asked, "So, what do you do all day if you can't go out until midnight?"

He pointed to the ragged deck of cards he'd moved to the edge of the table when they'd sat down.

"Poker?" she asked hopefully. "I'm good at poker."

"That's what my security team plays. But I think you and I should play something else. Something *I'm* good at."

She was almost afraid to ask. "What?"

He smiled and speared a bite of broccoli. "Hearts," he said.

Chapter Four

Kellen smiled blandly across the table. "I think War would be more appropriate. I want—"

She was interrupted midsentence by the sound of thundering footsteps in the hallway to the back door. Dominic was up instantly and reaching for her.

"Gordy's gone!" Spike announced as he stopped in the doorway, his face pale, his gun drawn.

"What do you mean 'gone'?" Burton, who had heard the commotion, stood in the doorway from the living room, gun also drawn.

"I mean he isn't there!" Spike snapped. "I went out to relieve him and he wasn't there. Some security hotshot you are! Mueller walked right in and took somebody out from under your nose."

Burton barked at Dominic. "Stay inside." Then he headed for the back door, Spike following.

Dominic pulled Kellen away from the window and into a corner between the wall and the refrigerator. He reached behind him and withdrew the 9mm Smith & Wesson.

Kellen, who just realized at that moment that she clutched his arm with both hands, released him and took a step back. "Is that loaded?" she asked.

"Wouldn't do us much good if it wasn't," he replied absently, pushing her farther into the corner as he kept an eye on the door.

"Of course," she replied, her voice a little high and breathless. "Stupid question. It's just that I'd never seen a real gun until I got here. And now I've seen so many."

He turned his attention to her for an instant, his eyes calm. "It's probably nothing."

Kellen wasn't convinced. She'd been in this house less than twelve hours, but she'd learned a few things for certain. "Gordy would never leave you voluntarily."

Dominic's expression tightened just a little and he turned his attention back to the door. "I know. But he might have seen something he wanted to investigate."

"Without Spike?"

Dominic turned to her again, a faint smile on his lips. "Relax. We don't know for certain that there's a problem yet."

"Hah," she scoffed, folding her arms, looking away from him because she was frightened and she didn't want him to see that in her eyes. "I was kidnapped, put to bed with a stranger and offered hot dogs for breakfast. Don't try to tell me there isn't a problem."

He laughed softly and reached out to touch her cheek. "That's because you were asleep the whole time we were in bed. Next time I'll wake you up, and you won't think of it as a problem anymore."

His eyes held hers for a moment, filled with warmth and interest and confident promise.

Then the back door opened and Dominic slipped in front of her, pressed back against her to conceal their presence, gun held down in both hands as he peered around the refrigerator. Kellen, on tiptoe to peer over Dominic's shoulder, prayed.

"It's us!" Burton shouted.

Dominic relaxed and stepped out into the room. "Any sign of Gordy?"

"No," Spike answered with a disdainful glance in the security man's direction. "Big man. Big bucks. And what did you do? You lost my partner!"

Burton rounded on him. "You were here, too! Did you see anything? Hear anything?"

"Hey, come on," Dominic said reasonably. "Who's responsible isn't the issue. The point is, he's gone. And it's doubtful he'd have gone willingly."

Spike shook his head. "Gordy wouldn't have left, even to check something out, without calling me first."

"Told you," Kellen said quietly to Dominic.

He silenced her with a sidelong glance.

Burton went to a radio placed incongruously on a pine, country-style hutch amid a collection of colorful Fiesta plates.

"Who's he calling?" Kellen asked quietly.

"Burton has men watching the highway," Dominic replied.

Burton got no response. He turned knobs, adjusted dials. Nothing. He looked at Dominic, then at Spike, his eyes bleak.

"That's it." Spike removed his pistol from its shoulder holster and checked the clip. "I'm taking Dominic out of here."

"You are not authorized..." Burton began, but Spike wasn't listening. He snapped the clip back in place and pushed Dominic toward the stairs. "Get warm clothes. We're running."

Spike pulled packaged food out of the cupboards and began dropping them into a duffel bag he retrieved from the rear hallway.

"They'll be waiting for you," Burton argued.

"It's better than being caught in here when he rushes the house."

Dominic took Kellen's hand and pulled her with him.

"We're not taking the little lady," Spike shouted after him. "She can go with Burton."

"No," Dominic stopped at the foot of the stairs to say the word simply, quietly. Kellen admired his style with it. His tone and the way he clipped the word suggested there was no argument against it. "She stays with me."

Spike moved away from the counter and straightened to his full height. "I'm not taking a woman on the run."

Dominic pushed her before him up the first step. "Then we're going on our own."

"Dominic," Kellen began, "maybe you should..."

He turned to her and pointed up to his room. A step apart they were eye to eye, and she could see no compromise in his. Their usual velvety darkness was like flint. "Go get your coat."

Still unable to quite believe what was happening despite Gordy's disappearance and the dead radio, she tried to take it calmly.

"I doubt that anyone has seen me. Why don't you just go with..."

His look finally stopped her. It remained implacable.

"And there's a woolen hat in my bottom drawer," he said. "Go."

She heard the argument resume as she ran into the bedroom to retrieve her long denim coat, and to find the hat.

She couldn't believe that angry male voices fought over whether or not she would accompany a world-famous true crime writer as he ran for his life. She took his black trench coat and the scarf he always wore and added them to the pile over her arm.

As an afterthought, she rummaged through the drawers and found socks. She removed two pairs and put one in each of their coat pockets.

"Does this mean you've been on the run before?"

She turned to find Dominic standing in the doorway. He leaned a forearm against the molding in an unconsciously graceful and dramatic pose that served to heighten her sense of unreality.

This wasn't theater, she told herself firmly, this was serious. Dominic was in grave danger, and it was no time for her to behave like a heartsick old maid.

"No, but I was a girl scout," she replied, pushing his coat and scarf at him. "Dry feet are essential to surviving outdoors."

He smiled. She looked elsewhere to protect herself from its impact.

"Good thinking. Although we'll be in the car."

"But you don't know where you'll end up."

"True."

She held a hand out and squared her shoulders. "Good luck. I've decided not to come with you."

He looked at her steadily. "Why?"

"Because I'm having trouble believing this is real," she said honestly, then added with a little more difficulty, "... and ... if I'm along Spike will be edgy and out of sorts and that might endanger you."

He raised an eyebrow. "And that concerns you?"

She averted her eyes on the pretense of brushing lint off the collar of her coat. "Of course. People are counting on you to put this Mueller behind bars and free an innocent man."

He reached out to lift her chin with his forefinger. "I don't believe that's the only reason," he said softly.

She fought an urge to turn her lips into his hand, to tell him it had been a wonderful if brief adventure and that she would never forget it or him, that it had gilded her quiet little life and somehow sharpened her. But he wouldn't leave her if she said that, and she truly did want him to stay safe.

"Then you're under a misapprehension," she answered coolly, returning his direct gaze.

He studied her another moment, then took her coat from her and held it open.

"I'm afraid you are, too," he replied.

She turned to slip her arms into the sleeves. "What's that?"

When she turned, buttoning her coat, he was shrugging into his.

"You seem to think you have a choice in the matter." He took her arm and pulled her with him toward the stairs. "You're coming with me."

"But..."

He ignored her long string of protests as she ran to keep up with him. Apparently Burton had decided to accompany them because he was following Spike into the garage with a small duffel that was tossed onto the floor in the backseat.

Burton held the front seat forward for her and Dominic urged her into the back. He followed her in. Burton held up a rifle that resembled something from "Top Cops." "You better with this or with the wheel?" he asked Spike.

Spike went around to the driver's side. "I have a lead foot and nerves of steel."

Burton took his place in the passenger seat.

"Ready?" Spike asked, the motor running, his hand poised over the garage door opener.

Dominic pulled Kellen down to the upholstery and covered her body with his. "Ready," he said.

Kellen heard the click of Burton's rifle, then the hum of the garage door as it slid up.

The spate of gunfire came as a complete surprise to Kellen. She'd half expected that they would leave the house without incident and that some highway patrolman would stop them halfway down the road and explain that Mueller had been apprehended before he'd even reached Oregon, and there was really no cause for alarm at all.

No such luck. The reality of their situation came home to Kellen when the continual popping of bullets exploded the rear window directly over them. Dominic leaned even closer over her, holding the front of his coat over her face.

She heard Burton return fire, felt the erratic, almost sickening sways and jerks of the car as Spike maneuvered like a stunt driver out of the long, winding driveway and onto the street.

It startled her to realize that despite the danger, the primary thought in her brain was *the Night Prince is shielding me with his body*. She was acutely aware of the weight of his long frame pressing hers into the upholstery, the soapy smell of him, the angular body structure under the rougher fabrics that said *man* in capital letters.

The car sped on in a straight line and everything was quiet for several minutes when Dominic rose cautiously off her. She tried to follow him up, but he pushed her down again.

"They're following," Spike reported, "but in another few minutes we're going to hit the interstate and traffic. If I can get far enough ahead, I can hide us off the road . . . somewhere."

"I know where," Kellen said, still pressed to the leather seat. "You turned north out of the driveway, didn't you?"

"He did," Dominic confirmed.

"Then in a few miles you'll be coming to a sign that says Fort Samson State Park. Take the turn and follow the signs to Battery Raymond."

Dominic, still leaning over her, turned her head slightly to look at her. "A fortification?"

"Built at the turn of the century. It's about a mile off the road, and there are tunnels where we can hide.

We might even be able to get the car in. It's usually deserted in the winter.''

"Good work, Kellen," Burton said in a strained voice.

Dominic brushed glass out of Kellen's hair with one hand while shielding her eyes with the other. "You're sure you've never been on the lam before?" he asked.

They drove for what felt like an eternity, speeding and swerving in an effort to stay well ahead of Mueller and his men. Then there was a victorious shout from Spike.

"Log truck cut 'em off," Spike announced. "He's..." There was a pause, then a loud exclamation.

"What?" Dominic demanded, still lying over Kellen.

"He ran off the road," Burton said in weak amazement.

Kellen judged by the sudden darkening inside the car that Spike had turned into the park with its two-lane road lined on both sides by tall trees.

Dominic pulled her up to a sitting position, but encouraged her to slouch down below the top of the seat.

Battery Raymond was completely deserted as Kellen had predicted. She directed them past the parking lot, through an entrance gate and up a hill intended for pedestrians.

The concrete frame of a deteriorating bunker stood just across a narrow green lawn. Graffiti marked the chipping concrete. Windowless rooms gaped at them, and two dark archways promised shelter. Spike drove carefully into one of them.

For a moment they sat in black silence, smells of dampness and decay penetrating the car.

Kellen sat up straight, brushed her hair back with her fingers and tried to form one coherent thought. She couldn't. She'd just been shot at with automatic weapons!

"Mueller must have brought all his cronies with him," Spike said.

"He's put an impressive team together," Dominic agreed. "All bright young men in his company used to wheeling and dealing and being the best. They're not accustomed to having a tidy profit pulled out from under them by a deal turned sour. They're ticked off and they're dangerous."

Kellen realized her contribution to their escape was only a stopgap measure. Now they had to get out of the park without being seen and get Dominic to safety while a car filled with Uzi-toting geniuses waited to reduce Burton's car and everyone in it to shrapnel.

"What do we do now?" she asked.

Before anyone could answer her, Burton fell sideways against Spike with a thunk. Spike shouted an expletive in the nearly complete darkness. "He's hit!"

Dominic stood to lean over the front seat, saw the spreading claret-colored stain on Burton's chest and shoulder and pressed his handkerchief to it as he added his own descriptive oath. He noticed only then that the passenger window was cracked and one perfect hole lined up with Burton's shoulder.

Burton winced and came to again. "Just my shoulder," he said, his voice low and thready. "I took it first thing out of the garage." He closed his eyes and moved his head restlessly. "Hell. I think I'm going to..."

He passed out before he could complete the thought.

Spike swore again.

"We have to get him to a hospital," Kellen said, leaning between the front seats, her face white.

Dominic pushed her back into her seat with his free hand.

"Spike, you stay with them." He reached forward to open the front door. "How far to a doctor, Kellen?"

"All the way into Astoria," she replied. "Or in the other direction to Sandpiper. You'll get caught!"

Spike supported Burton's unconscious body as Dominic pushed the seat forward enough to allow himself to slide out.

"Dominic, you ain't doin' that," Spike said with authority. "Even if Mueller is out of commission—and we don't know that he is, just that his car went off the road—the police might pick you up. The police commissioner in Massachusetts probably has an APB out for *you* for Bowles's murder. You gotta stay here."

"Burton needs—"

"I'm taking Burton for help." Spike opened his door, eased out of his seat and let Burton's body down gently. "I'm gonna find a place to call Rocco," he told Dominic over the top of the car, "then I'll be right back."

"Spike—"

"Hey!" Spike said sharply. "This is my call. This time you do what I say."

When Dominic would have quarreled with that, Spike reminded quietly, "You got two boys to get home to. Now do what I tell you. Help me get the gear out of the back.''

Kellen slid out of her seat to hold the bloody handkerchief in place over Burton's wound while Spike and Dominic hauled sleeping bags, a Primus stove, and the duffel of food out of the trunk of the car. She wondered why they were unloading the supplies if Spike was coming back with the car. Then the obvious answer presented itself. In case he didn't make it back.

Then Spike pulled Kellen out of the car and turned to Dominic. "Keep the little lady with you. She knows her way around here. That's important because Mueller doesn't.'' He turned to Kellen. "I'm counting on you to be as smart and as tough as you seem. Both of you stay undercover and don't even show your face outside. If they didn't damage the car, it won't be long before they're nosing around here. By then, I should be back with help.''

FROM THE MOUTH of the structure, Dominic and Kellen watched the bullet-pocked car with its blown-out window disappear out of sight as Spike, Burton slumped beside him, headed for the rear entrance to the park.

Kellen huddled into her coat, fighting the feeling that she had crossed into some weird and violent plane and was completely cut off from everyone and everything she had ever known.

Dominic took her arm and tried to pull her farther back into the concealing shelter of the structure. She shook him off.

He studied her set profile, the faint quiver at her lip, and guessed he was about to deal with an emotional blowup. Not precisely what he needed at the moment, though he could hardly blame her. He at least *wrote* about this kind of thing all the time, even if he didn't regularly live it. What had happened to her in the past twelve hours was probably relegated to television in her experience.

"Kellen," he said gently. "It's going to be all right." He touched her arm again and she turned on him, eyes bright with anger in the darkness.

"Gordy is missing, Burton's been shot, and we are hiding in an old fort with all the gear in case Spike doesn't make it back! Don't tell me it's going to be all right. I'm out of here and you can do whatever you think is right for you. You can explain it to Spike by saying I sneaked out on you while you were sleeping." She pointed into the darkness. "That leads into a tunnel system. Follow it, make a few turns, and just wait for Spike to come back."

She turned back to where the supplies had been placed and picked up the purse she had dropped there. She shouldered it as though this was just another walk to town.

Dominic followed her, then stopped behind her, a hand braced against the wall. When she turned, prepared to leave, their gazes clashed.

"Look," he began calmly. "I know what this is about."

She widened her eyes dramatically. "Do you? I'm so glad because, you know, I just arrived last night— in a blindfold, I might add." She tried to step around him, but he caught her arm.

"Kellen, you know I can't let you leave."

She surprised him when she nodded. "I know," she said amenably. Then she raised her free hand. "But I promise not to divulge your whereabouts if I'm captured and tortured. Unless, of course, they use chocolate deprivation, then you're pretty much on your own."

"Kellen . . ." he persisted reasonably.

She pulled against him, but he held fast. "I know how to get back home without being seen." Her voice raised a decibel as she pulled harder. "There's a phone just a mile back at the junction. I have a friend I can call to . . ."

He saw the storm of emotion in her eyes and wished she would just let it out. Betsy had been just like that, using cleverness and anger to cloak fear and tears.

He backed her up against the damp, rough concrete wall. The words died on her lips and her eyes grew large, green as emerald and with the same fire. Good. His distraction tactics hadn't rusted in the two years since Betsy.

"I know what you experienced was frightening," he said, "but I won't let anything happen to you." He lowered his lips toward hers. "I care about you."

"Dominic Hunter, if you kiss me . . ." she threatened, both fists pushing with all her strength against his chest.

He caught her wrists in his hands and pressed them to the wall on either side of her. Her resistance was fervent but ineffective. For a minute he let himself savor the anticipation.

Under the blue denim, her small breasts rose and fell with the pace of her fury.

She turned her face away as he lowered his head. "I don't want you to kiss me," she said angrily. *"Don't kiss me."*

"Right." He placed his cheek against the side of her face, all he could touch of her, and rubbed gently.

He felt her draw in a strangled little breath even before the sound blew softly into his ear. "I said . . ."

"Not to kiss you. I heard you. This isn't a kiss." As he spoke, he rubbed his jaw against her cheekbone and her temple.

She turned her face to avoid him. Gently, he assaulted her other cheek.

"Stop," she whispered, gasping again as he nipped gently at the rim of her ear.

"In a minute," he whispered back.

He was placing kisses down the side of her neck. He wasn't certain but he suspected she leaned away from him to allow him access rather than to escape him.

Kellen had never been this confused. Or this angry. Or this desperate to be kissed.

But there was a principle at stake here. She couldn't quite define what it was, but she was sure it was important.

"You're hurting me," she lied, needing urgently to put some distance between them before she succumbed to his seduction.

He loosened his hold fractionally and, thinking he meant to release her, she turned her face to look into his eyes. Big mistake. They were dark and inviting, like his kisses felt, and the need to struggle against him intensified.

"Whether or not I let you go," he said gravely, "depends on what you plan to do."

"I plan to go home."

"Then we're going to have to spend the next few days just like this."

"Dominic, this isn't funny," she tried to say firmly. The words came out low and thin.

He grinned. "Good. That was never my intention."

She met his gaze steadily, her eyes troubled and dark. "This also isn't *real,*" she said, a trace of desperation in her voice.

He heard it and freed her. He lowered his own hands to his hips and frowned. "What do you mean?"

She leaned back against the wall and drew in a big damp, dank gulp of air. "I mean I refuse to become part of it. I came here by accident, and though it was a little exciting, it was also infuriating and scary, and it wasn't really supposed to happen." She reminded him bleakly, "You were angry that they'd brought me, remember?"

He nodded, putting a hand to her cheek. "That was last night. Right now, selfishly, I'm very glad you're here."

"You have ulterior motives for saying that," she accused.

"I said it because it's true. Because it's *real.*"

"You said it," she corrected, "because you want to kiss me."

His dark gaze looked into her eyes, their depths clear to him even in the darkness. "You want me to kiss you," he said softly.

She didn't deny it, simply straightened away from the wall with a determined expression on her face. "And that is precisely why I'm leaving."

Chapter Five

Experience had taught Dominic that this was where it got difficult with a woman. When things ceased making sense. When what was expressed wasn't really what she meant at all.

Clever maneuvering was required here. He hoped he hadn't lost the knack.

"You have it all wrong," he countered. "You aren't here by accident. By mistake, maybe, but not by accident."

She rolled her eyes. They looked a little less desperate, he noticed with satisfaction, though no less angry. "Please don't play word games with me. As a writer, you have an unfair advantage." She frowned, folding her arms. "And what does that mean, anyway?"

He was warming to the challenge. Matters of life and death seemed to recede in importance. Reaching the heart of this woman was suddenly all that mattered. He gave the effort every particle of his considerable research and storytelling skills.

"If you'll recall how you came to be with me in the first place," he began, "you'll remember it was because I chose you. Spike and Gordy made a big mistake bringing you to me, but it was no accident. They heard me express my deepest desire at that moment—and that was you.''

''I'm flattered, really,'' she said. And I'm intrigued and attracted and desirous of you myself. ''But I'm also terrified. I hate to be the one to tell you this, but being attracted to you is like flirting with death! It means the possibility of bullet holes in your body!''

He folded his arms and let her go on, knowing it would be futile at this point to try to stop her.

''Men are chasing you at high speeds and shooting out the windows of your car! They're wounding your friends! Some high-powered lunatic chased you all the way across the country.''

She hesitated long enough that he thought she was finished. He opened his mouth to speak, but she raised a hand.

''No, don't try to placate me. This isn't hysteria, this is simple common sense. I do *not* have a death wish. I envision a long and fruitful life, and I'm not going to have it if I stay with you.''

He tried to appeal to her sympathy. ''So, you'd leave me here alone?'' He swept a hand around their dark surroundings.

''Please,'' she said dryly. ''You're hardly helpless. In fact, without me, you'll have less to worry about.''

''You think I won't worry about you,'' he asked, running his hand gently down the arms of her denim coat, ''just because you're not with me. I wrote one paragraph last night that I finally deleted because I kept looking at you asleep on my sofa. So I took you to bed, and you know what happened?''

She was afraid to ask. She had a vague impression she'd been pushing aside all morning.

He caught her hands and held them. "You behaved, even in your sleep, as though you belonged there."

She tried to pull her hands away but he held firm. "Something happened between us the moment we saw each other through that store window, Kellen," he said softly. "You know it did."

He was absolutely right, but that couldn't be. It couldn't possibly be. She tugged on her hands again and this time he let her go. She turned away from him. "Maybe I was living out a girlish dream that a handsome prince would appear out of the darkness and whisk me off to some faraway kingdom."

"Connecticut's not that far. And twenty acres is hardly a kingdom."

She shook her head. "I have to get back to my real life."

She tried to walk past him, but he stopped her again, holding her firmly by the shoulders.

"All right, pay attention," he said, when she looked up at him, big-eyed with surprise. "I'm not going to deny ulterior motives here, but there's something else you have to learn about our situation, and right now."

He pulled her to him and kissed her thoroughly. With the artful use of tongue and teeth and the encouragement of his wandering hands, he brought her out of surprise, out of the fear and confusion she'd felt at Mueller's frightening pursuit, and into the very immediate drama of the moment.

Dominic took her lips with such complete control of the encounter that Kellen could do little at first but simply accept him. His tongue traced the startled and open line of her mouth, the rim of her teeth, then invaded deeper, seeming to reach right down inside her.

Without air to breathe or space to move, she stood pliant in his arms and what she'd been so sure was only fantasy came slowly, firmly to life.

She felt it come from deep inside her, the response he was reaching for, the need to make heart-to-heart contact she'd tried so hard to ignore.

As he moved to nibble at her lips, her jaw, her ear, she kissed his chin, his cheek, the thrumming pulse at his temple.

Then his mouth was on hers once again and she met it urgently, kissing him back with all the fervor of the storybook tale—with the magic that awakened each of them.

Dominic was a little surprised to find himself breathless when he drew away, to find that her response had lighted a fire in him that he banked with considerable difficulty.

"Did that feel unreal to you?" he demanded. He took her hand and placed it over his heart. He knew by the way it rocketed in his chest she would feel it through his sweater and coat. "Is this a fantasy?"

Kellen still felt the imprint of his lips and hands everywhere they had touched her, and his heart beat against her hand with strong life.

She wasn't sufficiently recovered from his kiss to answer him.

"I'm real," he said gravely. "You're real. And wherever life places us, no matter how plotlike the situation, that's reality. Fate brought you to me, not Spike and Gordy."

She looked around at the darkness of the tunnel surrounding them.

"Don't you see how dangerous this could be?" she asked urgently. "And I'm not talking about crazy people chasing you and bullets flying. I mean . . ." she flattened a slender hand over her heart ". . . personal danger. We're already...attracted...and it's only been hours. What do you think several days confined together will do to that?"

"I'm anxious to find out."

She shook her head, smiling thinly with impatience and a growing sense of fatalism. "And then what?"

He pulled her back into his arms, rubbing gently between her shoulder blades. "I think the best way to answer that is to just let it happen."

She was caving. He dropped his hands from her and said with a carefully calculated combination of nonchalance and sincerity, "Anyway, the present is going to take all our wit and resourcefulness. Right now, I need you for your knowledge of the area. If Spike doesn't get back, I'm not willing to sit in here forever. And two heads are always better than one."

He offered his hand. "So, what do you say? Can we just put all this aside until Mueller's out of the way and we can resume normal life again? Will you stay with me?"

Kellen considered him a long moment. His eyes were sincere and what he asked was only reasonable. But she had a bad feeling about it. She could live with the prince for a few days—or however long it took to find Mueller—but she couldn't dispel the feeling that there was a poisoned apple in here somewhere.

Still, she took his hand. She wasn't ready yet to go back to the other side of the window.

THEY MOVED THEIR sleeping bags, stove and food around a bend in the tunnel so that they could use the flashlight Spike had also left with them.

"Where does the tunnel go?" Dominic asked, flashing it around the floor and walls.

"To a lookout onto the ocean," Kellen replied.

"Come on." He took her hand. "Let's check it out."

Close together, they followed the winding tunnel around several turns. At the last turn, they could feel the wind, and hear the distant surf. The salty smell of it wafted around them. Then a small, open square in the concrete where the nose of a cannon once stood, framed a cloudy blue sky. On the other side of the room, a low guard rail protected a wide hole that wound down into the darkness.

Kellen went to the opening and inhaled the fresh air as though they'd been in the tunnel days instead of just an hour. She leaned out and let the wind sweep her mind clean of fear, concern and confusion. They were relatively safe, and time had slowed to a crawl; the best thing to do was relax and go with it.

Dominic was pleased to see the lines of her jaw and her shoulders soften. Continued tension and anger would be hard to deal with under the circumstances. Then she turned to smile at him, and his heart did a little flip. He suddenly wasn't sure that Kellen in a co-operative mood would be any easier on his nerves.

"Doesn't this make you feel like we're half the Ninja Turtle team," she asked, turning to the opening again, her hair streaming behind her in the breeze, "waiting for a pizza delivery to our cozy sewer abode?"

He came behind her and looked over her shoulder. The ocean was about a quarter of a mile away beyond knee-high grass.

"No," he replied, "I have trouble thinking of turtles in heroic terms. I'd rather think of myself as your Night Prince. With a little imagination, our setting is appropriate. You could be looking over the battlements right now, waiting for me to return with my army from a meeting with the king."

She looked down then over her shoulder at him with another smile. "There's no drawbridge over the moat."

"I'm a good swimmer."

"You're probably wearing armor. You'll go down like a stone."

"You'll swan-dive in to save me, won't you?"

"It wouldn't help. I don't know how armor comes off."

Somehow, the notion of her giving thought to taking anything off him, even imaginary armor, suddenly charged the air around him. And they'd shaken hands on putting all that off until the danger was past.

He took her hand and pulled her away from the opening. "We have to do something about firewood."

"Right next door." She tugged him to the small room just beyond the wall. "They hold demonstrations here in the summer to show how the men lived. They always have a fire going in the fireplace. And farther down and at a right angle are the public rest-rooms."

"Well, my, my," he said, turning the light close to her to light her face without blinding her. "Indoor plumbing in our castle, and possibly even kindling."

"Hey, am I a good little housekeeper, or what?"

"You are indeed. I guess I won't trade you to the Vikings for mead."

"Are they still around?" she asked. "What century is this, anyway?"

"I'm not sure. I believe the Vikings turned to Christianity at the end of the tenth century. And William the Conqueror was a descendant of Hrolf the Ganger. That about sums up my knowledge of the subject."

"I suppose if you're not going to trade me," she said, laughing softly, "it really doesn't matter. Fantasies don't have to be reality-based anyway, do they?"

He shook his head. "You're right. Dealing in fact as I do, I forget that sometimes you can just make things up. Is this what you were talking about?" He swung the light around the small room.

"Yes." She spotted a rough wooden box on the floor. Dominic flashed the light on it and she flipped up the hinged lid. The fragrance of cedar wafted up from neatly cut and placed kindling.

She reached in to hold up a piece for Dominic to see. Then she caught sight of a large black spider crawling off the cedar and onto the sleeve of her coat.

With a scream and a jump backward, she dropped the piece of wood and swatted at her sleeve. The spider fell and scurried away. She shuddered and wrapped her arms around herself.

Smiling gently, Dominic put an arm around her and pulled her close to his side. "Not a spider lover, eh?"

She shuddered against him again, letting herself absorb the security he represented. "No. Is anybody?"

"I'm afraid my younger son is."

Kellen thought he spoke the words apologetically, as though one day she might have to deal with the fact that his son liked spiders and she didn't.

"Let's check out the restrooms," she suggested, pushing out of his arms. "I'd love to splash water on my face."

"All right. Lead on."

"PATÉ?" KELLEN HELD the flashlight on the small round can she'd pulled out of their duffel and stared at it in disbelief. She read from the label. "Swiss vegetarian paté with herbs and tomato."

Dominic, smoothing out one of the sleeping bags to use as a kind of cushion, expressed approval. They had moved into the small room with the fireplace. "Good. Doesn't require cooking, so we can save the firewood for dinner and warmth. Any crackers?"

Kellen directed the light inside the duffel. "We have a couple of apples, a bag of cheese curls, a can of soup, a can of stew, paper plates. A Primus stove. No coffee, but a few cans of Coke and..."

He turned to her with a mournful expression. "No coffee?"

"No," she replied. "But would you believe we have a box of Captain Krunch and a jar of olives?"

He looked more cheerful. "Green or black?"

She turned the light on him, her lips pursed in disapproval. "We're caught in a life-and-death situation with kids' cereal and a jar of olives and you want to know what kind they are?"

He placed the second sleeping bag against the wall as a rear cushion and waved her to join him.

"You're not very good at this fantasy stuff, are you?" he asked. He took the duffel from her and patted the place beside him. "It can be very magical if you have the right attitude."

"Magical? Well, I hope you have something up your sleeve—like crackers—because there aren't any in the bag."

She sat beside him as he put the bag between his bent knees and studied the contents. "I thought for sure we had a loaf of cocktail rye. Ah. Here it is."

He removed the foot-long loaf of tiny dark slices.

"Got a knife?" she challenged.

"Of course," he replied, turning toward her to reach into his hip pocket.

His size and his warmth enveloped her for a heady moment, then he produced a pocketknife with a smug grin.

"Thought you had me there, didn't you? But guys always carry a knife. It's a male thing, you know. A symbol of our toughness, our preparedness."

Kellen heaved a dramatic little sigh. "My hero. Had I been stuck here alone I'd have had to dip cheese curls in my paté."

"Very uncivilized."

"Actually," she admitted as he handed her a plate with several slices covered with the aromatic spread, "I've never had paté."

He popped the top on a can of Coke and handed it to her. "I don't like most snob foods, but paté is delicious. Usually not good for your arteries, I guess, but this stuff's vegetarian."

She took a careful bite, chewed, and had to agree. It was delicious.

"When was the last time you had the real thing?" she asked.

"Umm..." He chewed and thought. "At a reception in New York City, I think. Last summer."

She could imagine a luxurious spread of food and elegantly garbed New Yorkers talking and laughing around it.

"A reception for whom?"

He popped the last bite into his mouth and pointed to himself.

"For you?" she asked, her image of the glittery event placing him in the middle.

He nodded and took a swig from his can of cola. "For my last book," he said, putting the can aside.

"What were you wearing?"

He raised an eyebrow in surprise. "Why?"

"Because I'm creating a mental picture. A white suit like you see in pictures of men in the Hamptons on Long Island?"

"God, no," he said, laughing softly at the idea. "It was black-tie. Usually, my uniform is a pair of old jeans and maybe a disreputable sportscoat. The occasional autograph party or reception unfortunately requires me to wear something more formal."

Her mind's eye put him in tie and tails. For a moment, her mind ceased to function. It could only stare. He looked wonderful, tall and broad and straight, dark hair slicked back, stubborn waves forming at his side part. When she saw herself there, she shook her head and forced herself back to reality. Or what he insisted was reality. She still wasn't sure.

"Your life must be very exciting," she said.

He chuckled. "You mean like now?"

She had to laugh, too. "I mean under normal circumstances. World famous writer, fancy receptions, probably talk-show appearances."

"It's interesting," he conceded. "But it's more satisfying than exciting. The research can be very tedious, as can some of the people who come to my receptions. Autographings are always fun, though. It's a revelation to meet your readers and learn just what it is they really like about your work."

Her bread and paté gone, she turned toward him, knees bent. "Why are people so fascinated with the grisly details of that kind of story? I mean, obviously your approach must make it interesting if you sell millions of copies, but why do you think people want to read about brutal killers?"

He frowned, bracing an arm on one knee and dangling the pop can from his hand. "This is just my theory based on what my readers tell me," he qualified, "but I think they're as interested in what brought someone to that point where murder was a choice, as they are in how it was done."

"I was hoping it was more than morbid curiosity."

He smiled thinly. "Well, there's that, too. Morbid curiosity is an intrinsic part of us. You can't raise a couple of young boys and not realize that. But I think the fascination with crime goes way beyond that. I think actually planning a murder is so foreign to the average person, that he wants to understand what could bring someone else to do it.''

"What does make them do it?"

"Usually they're sociopaths who know the difference between right and wrong but consider themselves special enough to be beyond the rules. And usually that behavior is brought about by having been subjected to brutality as children.''

"And knowing the details yourself doesn't haunt your dreams?''

He shook his head. "No. In fact, there's a kind of comfort in knowing that kind of thing has never touched your life or the lives of those you love. And, of course, I've met a lot of heroes in my research—the cops and district attorneys who find these people and put them away.''

"And in this particular case," she added, "you'll save someone who's been wrongly convicted.''

He nodded, quiet for a moment. She placed a hand on his arm, suspecting that for some reason he needed comfort.

"It must have been frightening to have this case turn on you like this," she guessed.

He placed his hand over hers, applying the smallest pressure that expressed appreciation for her understanding. "Actually, it scared the hell out of me because I had all those kids with me at the time.''

"The pizza party for your son's birthday," she recalled. "You said you overpowered the man.''

"I knocked him out," he said, teasingly defensive.

Deciding he needed the mood lightened, she taunted back. "Apparently not very well. He got up and left.''

"Who's telling this story?''

"I'm sorry. Do continue."

"That's pretty much it. The boys were streaming into the house and I'd stayed behind to lock the van and set the alarm, and as I turned away I saw something move behind me through the side mirror. I ducked. He missed. And I tackled him and hit him."

She shook her head slowly. "I live such a dull life in comparison." Then she laughed. "That is, I did until I was brought home to you." She grew serious again suddenly. "How do you suppose Mueller trailed you all the way out here?"

Dominic shrugged. "Burton, Gordy and I took a commercial flight out of Hartford while my uncle took another flight with my boys. Some ticket clerk might have remembered me even though I used an assumed name. Same thing probably happened with the local airline that flew us out here from Portland. Mueller's got the police commissioner's cooperation, remember?"

Dominic's explanation was punctuated by a loud roar from the end of the tunnel through which they'd come in. They froze into silence and he flipped off the flashlight.

The sound swelled, and seemed to fill every twist of the tunnel. Kellen reached for Dominic, unable to determine what the sound was. Was a plane about to crash on them? Was this what an earthquake sounded like from right above it?

Then the sound slowed and quieted and finally stopped.

Dominic placed a hand over Kellen's mouth and pulled her close, wondering what the hell a motorcycle was doing in the tunnel. Unless it belonged to one of Mueller's men, but if that were the case, certainly he'd have come in force rather than alone. So, who was this?

He had his answer a moment later. Firstly, he'd been wrong. The intruder was not alone. A high, feminine voice cooed as the sound of creaking leather, probably being removed, rounded the dark corner of the tunnel.

Secondly, it took less than several seconds to decide that this was an impromptu, lustful moment that apparently couldn't wait for the next motel.

"Slash, you are so bad!" the female voice cooed. "I mean what if..." There was the sound of fabric tearing. "Ooh, baby!"

Kellen's forehead thunked against Dominic's shoulder and he lowered his face to her neck to stifle the laughter he wasn't sure he could contain.

He had to admire Slash's stamina. The oohs and aahs went on and on until a satisfied little female sigh ended the event.

Leather creaked once more, then in a very disgruntled voice the lady asked, "Now what am I supposed to wear while we're riding sixty-five miles to Longview? I admit I have the finest one from here to the Follies Bergere, but what are you going to tell the officer when he pulls you over because my bare..."

The bike roared to life. Dominic pressed his hand over Kellen's ear as the sound exploded around them. He couldn't help but wonder if the biker had found a solution to the lady's problem or just got tired of listening to it. Either way, he wished he could watch them ride away.

When the sound of the motorcycle finally died, Kellen leaned away from Dominic, laughing hysterically.

"Do you believe that happened?" she demanded, choking as she gasped for breath.

He slapped her on the back, finally freeing his own laughter so that he was unable to reply.

She punched him lightly on the shoulder, still laughing. "And it didn't help that you were laughing in my ear. I thought for sure we were going to ruin everything for them by bursting into guffaws."

"Hey, I doubt they'd have even noticed us."

"Oh, my." Kellen sighed as they leaned back against the wall, side by side, hilarity spent. "You do have a way with building your fantasies, Dominic. This was another first for me. Let me tell you that dressing windows was never like this."

"Stick with me, woman. My life's a thrill a minute."

Kellen's stomach grumbled. She put a hand to it and rolled her head to look at Dominic. "I'm still hungry. Want to share an apple?"

He turned to grin at her. "That's a loaded question."

"That was Adam and Eve," she said, "not Dominic and Kellen." She began to root through the bag.

Dominic wandered toward the bend in the cave.

"Where you going?" Kellen asked.

"Reconnoitering," he replied. "Stay there."

Dominic walked all the way to the entrance and back, pausing far enough from the opening that he wouldn't be seen by anyone outside.

Their recent experience with the biker and his girl had had its amusing side, but the fact that someone had come into the tunnel made him wonder how often people did wander in and out even if the park wasn't much used in the winter.

And on the heels of that thought, he wondered what Burton and Spike were up to. Whether they'd found Gordy, and discovered what had happened to Burton's men. Whether Spike had made contact with Rocco.

He also thought about his boys and let himself feel the ache separation from them caused. God, but he wanted his life back to normal!

A hand came around him from behind, holding an apple.

He turned to Kellen, thinking that she did make him feel as though a part of his life that had been closed off was being reborn—new and fresh.

"May I use your knife?" she asked, then frowned at him. "Something wrong? I mean, other than the fact that someone's trying to kill you, you miss your kids, and you're stuck in a tunnel in the boondocks with a strange woman?"

"No. Nothing's wrong." He took the apple from her, gave it a toss in the air, then hooked his free arm around her neck and started back toward their little nook. "In fact," he said, squeezing her to him, "one or two things are very right."

Chapter Six

The scream curdled his blood. It reached right into the dark well of his dreamless sleep and brought him bolt upright.

For an instant he was disoriented. The darkness was so complete. He knew he wasn't at home. But where was the light? Since he'd been holed up at the "safe" house, he worked all night and slept during the day— or tried to. He was continually awakened by the pervasive daylight.

Then he heard the scream again, right beside him, and felt a leg flail against him, a hand fling out and strike his arm. Then it came back to him. Kellen. The tunnel.

He turned to reach for her at the same moment that she, too, bolted up. She came into his arms, a scream on her lips that died as she awoke. She shuddered and brushed frantically at her body.

"Kellen." He caught her arms and stilled her movement. She fought against him for a moment, then stopped, still trembling. "You had a bad dream. It's all right." He pulled her into his arms and smiled into the darkness. "Well, I mean, all things considered, it's all right."

She wrapped her arms around him and held tightly, burrowing her face in his shoulder. She groaned, her voice small and muffled. "There were spiders all over me. How can I accept flying bullets with equanimity, and have a nightmare over one spider?"

"It's the complicated female psyche," he said, laughter in his voice. He had to think about laughter. The way she was holding him, her soft breasts through her open coat pressed against his chest.

They'd zipped the two sleeping bags together and settled down for the night side by side, accepting without discussion that it was the practical way to keep warm and a necessity enforced by their situation.

But they'd had enough room to lie on their backs, nothing touching but their shoulders and, occasionally, a sock-clad foot. It had been no big deal.

But now it was. He knew many contemporary women would neither understand nor approve, but a vulnerable woman turned his resolve to jelly and his protective instincts to oak.

"And what do you know about the complicated female psyche?" she asked, not moving, except to snuggle closer.

Pulling away didn't occur to him. He simply held her and rubbed her back. He could feel her stiff spine relaxing under his hand.

"Ah . . ." He had to play the question over in his mind. He knew he'd heard it, but it hadn't registered. Right. The female psyche. "Mostly that it's a mass of contradictions."

"I'm not sure, but I think that's a sexist thing to say."

"Probably is," he agreed. "But it's my contention that we're all more sexist than current popular opinion considers proper. We were created to be different from one another, to provide what the other lacks and enhance what the other possesses."

At the moment, Kellen couldn't take serious issue with that. She needed to be held, and she was more than pleased that he had strong arms and the protective instinct with which to oblige her.

Finally composed, she drew back and said with a rueful sigh, "I hate to be like the difficult child on a trip, but I have to go to the bathroom."

He was grateful for an excuse to get up and walk around. "I'll walk you."

"I'll be fine if you'll let me take the flashlight."

"No. I'll check it out for you first. Might be critters around at this time of night."

She punched his shoulder. "Don't say that."

"You know, that's the second time you've done that," he remarked, reaching for the light he'd left beside him, and helping her to her feet. "I yell at my boys for hitting."

"I apologize," she said. He flashed the light near her face and doubted her sincerity. She was grinning. She laughed outright when he caught her. "Well, some things just call for a punch. Certainly that rocklike shoulder can take it. I suppose you have a Nautilus in your kingdom far away?"

With an arm around her shoulders, he lighted their path and started for the tunnel opening.

"No. I do go to a gym, though, right after I drop the boys off at school. It clears my mind to write."

"I don't work out," she admitted guiltily, "but I spend most of my time climbing in and out of windows, moving heavy stuff around. After that, I'm too worn out to exercise anyway."

He laughed. "Makes you sound like a second-story man."

At the mouth of the tunnel, Dominic held her back while he checked the compound, then quickly checked the ladies' room.

"Free of critters," he announced.

"CAN'T WE STAY OUT for just a minute?" she cajoled when she returned. "I know it's cold, but there doesn't seem to be anyone around and the night air is so refreshing."

He looked as though he intended to refuse her, then thought better of it. "Okay, just a few minutes. But stay close to the tunnel."

Not that he was anxious to crawl back into the sleeping bag with her, unable to touch her. But he felt sharply the responsibility for her safety, since she was in danger because of him in the first place.

He wished he knew whether Spike hadn't come back because he'd gotten Burton to safety and called Rocco, or because they'd failed. Uncertainty made him tense.

Kellen drew in deep gulps of air. Though the night was cold and damp, the clean air in her lungs felt wonderful and, after the darkness of the tunnel, served to dispel all remnants of her nightmare.

In fact, she felt as though it put her on an even emotional keel. Those few minutes after the nightmare, wrapped in Dominic's arms, she'd been close to slipping into the spell of the fantasy, into accepting it as reality. But, outside of the tunnel, things seemed to balance themselves once again. The danger in which she found herself was real, but the seductive pull of Dominic Hunter was made out of the shadows of the night and her own loneliness.

It seemed important to wedge a space between them before they had to go back to that sleeping bag.

"I've been to Connecticut," she said lightly, conversationally, huddled into her coat as she paced the width of the tunnel opening.

Dominic heard a subtle argumentative quality in her voice. It might have surprised him because she'd been happy enough to have him hold her only moments before. But right now he was a mass of raw nerves himself and primed to deal with it.

"Really." That was not a question because he knew she was about to explain.

She paced in her denim coat, hands jammed in her pockets. He almost couldn't remember what she looked like under the damn thing.

"I told you my mother writes travel books."

He nodded.

"She was doing one on New England between my senior year in high school and my first year of college."

"What did you think of it?"

"I thought," she said, her air pontifical, "that there seemed to be a lot of snobbish people who commuted to New York for their jobs, but made so much money they could live in exclusive neighborhoods, buy a lot of chintz and twig furniture for their fancy homes and call it country." She paused in the act of pacing to challenge quietly, "I'm surprised you'd want to raise children there."

This was going to be harder than he'd thought. The need for action tingled everywhere in his body. Instead, he replied calmly, "I have a comfortable home in a beautiful valley. And the last time I walked through, there wasn't one item of chintz or twig. I do have a pine cabinet and an oak dresser, but my grandfather made both of them and I don't think I'll chop them to kindling because you might mistake them for country affectation."

He closed the small space that separated them to stop within an inch of her and look down on her grimly. "I'm raising my boys there because Betsy and I spent a long weekend in the town and fell in love with it. We saved for years to get enough money to make a down payment on a beautiful piece of land near a lake. And I'm raising my boys there because they love horses and dogs and trees."

She wanted to kick herself. "I didn't mean..." she began defensively.

He talked over her. "We have a doctor on one side of us, and a studio photographer on the other. I suppose they're not your classic small-town types, and the photographer does sometimes commute to New York, but I've never thought of either of them as snobbish."

"Dominic—"

"In fact, if I were to attach that quality to someone, it would be to a young woman who's spent so much of her time creating artificial scenes in store

windows that she no longer has any concept of what
real life is all about.''

She looked up at him, anger and remorse warring in
her eyes. Then she spun on her heel and stormed back
into the tunnel.

He grabbed the arm of her coat and turned her
around. She glared up at him, defiant, regretful,
waiting.

He took her hand and slapped the flashlight into it.
''You'll need this,'' he said.

He was both pleased and concerned that that **obvi**-
ously hadn't been the reaction she'd wanted.

She turned again and disappeared down the dark
tunnel like a wraith, the light glowing out ahead of
her.

Then he paced, trying to get himself together. For a
man who liked things his way, he was frustrated on so
many levels that he felt the fragile seal on his control
beginning to break. He wanted his kids, he wanted his
life back, he wanted to get on with his book—and he
wanted Kellen with a single-mindedness that was going to compromise his alertness to danger and his
ability to react if he didn't do something about it soon.

He walked off steam for another few minutes, then
went back into the tunnel, resolved to have this out
with her. He knew why she was charming one moment and rude the next—she felt just as he did. Maybe
the best solution was to deal with the situation.

Prepared to do just that, he groaned as he reached
their sparse accommodations of sleeping bag and
groceries. She'd left the light on for him to guide his
steps, but she was asleep.

He'd hoped that would happen when he'd let her go back ahead of him. He'd wanted the time alone to calm down, to remind himself that other priorities had to take precedence over his desperate longing for the woman he'd found in a shop window.

But it was so easy to elbow common sense aside when he thought about holding her in his arms, about rising over her and opening a world for them where nothing existed but the two of them—no threats, no problems, no irreconcilable plans for the future.

That time would come, he was sure, but it wouldn't be tonight. He accepted that as he pulled off his shoes, wrapped his coat around him and slid into the bag beside her. She lay far to one side, hands curled under her chin. She'd put on the hat he'd had her bring, but she was huddled down, a frown between her eyebrows as though she were uncomfortable.

Resigned to another night of physical and emotional distress, he turned her into his arms, tucked the top of the bag around her shoulders and held her tightly to him.

She made a little sound of contentment and hiked a leg up against him. With a groan, he made himself lie still.

KELLEN AWOKE to the aroma of something cooking. The quality of the tunnel's darkness had changed. She guessed it must be daylight.

A motley collection of questions struck her as she sat up. Had Dominic come to bed? Was he still angry with her? Why on earth had she tried to pick a fight by attacking his home and his performance as a parent? Where was Spike? For that matter, where was Gordy?

Had things gone wrong? If they had, what were she and Dominic to do now? And did he still even include her in his escape?

Slipping out of the sleeping bag required all the self-control she possessed. She found Dominic warming the can of soup on the Primus stove set up on the cannon mount. His quick glance at her and his clipped "Good morning," answered two of her questions. Yes, he was still angry. And since he'd set out two paper plates, he probably did still consider her part of the escape plan; but he wasn't thrilled about it. She couldn't blame him.

"Good morning," she replied. "Smells good."

He gave her a very brief nod. "Thought I'd save the firewood to keep us warm. Eating soup with our fingers is going to be a challenge. I'll put the vegetables on the plates and leave the broth in the can to drink."

She forced a cheerful smile. "We can scoop up the vegetables with the cocktail rye. Do you still have the can from the stew we had last night?"

He pointed to it with his knife.

"I'll clean it out and fill it with water in the ladies' room. Then we can boil water in it for tea."

He frowned. "We don't have tea."

"I do," she announced smugly. "I always have a few bags in my purse. If I'm desperate when I'm working late and the shop I'm doing doesn't have a coffeepot, hot water from the tap will make a reasonable cup."

"Great," he said. He did not seem impressed either with her resourcefulness or with her.

She started to walk away with the can, then stopped at the bend in the cave. She turned back to him, squaring her shoulders.

"Look, I'm sorry about those things I said last night. I was being thoughtless and stupid. I—I'd been frightened and you—you—oh, God!" *I'm falling in love with you and I'm afraid if we get too close we'll do something we can't take back, then this will all work out and you'll go your way and I'll go mine and it makes me really crabby to think about it.* Sure. He was bound to understand that.

"I'll get the water," she told him, and disappeared down the tunnel.

Dominic watched her go, brooding bad temper filling every corner of his being. He'd slept about a total of an hour after he'd crawled back into the bag with her last night. She'd slept soundly on his shoulder, her hand moving over his chest, her leg nudging up and down his as she slept. He would doze off to awaken with her cheek against his, or her upper body sprawled across his chest, or her arm hooked over him.

He was a physical and emotional wreck this morning, and he hoped to God nothing happened that would require quick thinking or reflexive action on his part.

Water boiled on the little stove while they ate in silence.

"Do you think Spike and Burton are okay?" she asked.

He hesitated a moment before he answered. "Probably. But something's preventing Spike from getting back and I'm getting more and more concerned about my kids."

She frowned, catching his concern without understanding it. "Why?"

"Because if Mueller found me, he could find them. And they'd be just the way to get to me."

She put a hand on his arm as she had yesterday afternoon. "I'm sure it's just your mind working overtime. Your boys are with your uncle, aren't they?"

"I won't rest easy until I talk to them." Ignoring her hand, he stood and went to check the can of water. "You said your place is on the beach."

He'd closed a door between them this morning. Kellen accepted it with a sigh. "Yes."

"We'll wait until dark," he said, using the tail of his coat to remove the can from the fire. He brought it to the stone shelf where she sat and she dropped a battered-looking tea bag into it. "Then we'll head that way."

She tried to sip the tea, but found it too hot. She passed it back to him. "It's a good ten or fifteen-mile walk," she warned. "And unless you want to walk along the highway, which you probably don't, it'll be an even longer walk along the beach. And there's an isthmus in Gearhart before you get to Sandpiper, that'll send us back to the road."

His look was bland and even. "I thought you told me when you wanted to run out on me that it would be easy for you to get home."

"At that point," she admitted, annoyed with his remoteness, "a ten-mile walk on the sand would have been preferable to staying here."

He didn't take offense. Nothing changed in his expression. He simply sipped at the steaming can of tea, then passed it back to her. "Live and learn. I should have let you go."

She sipped at the scalding tea for fortification, then handed it back to him and stood.

"Then there's no reason we should make this trip together, is there?" she demanded. "In fact, if it weren't for the need to make contact with your boys, who are probably very nice and can't help that they're related to you, I'd damn well make you find someplace else to go even if your life *is* in danger. So, you go your way, I'll go mine and I'll meet you there."

"That's absurd." He took another sip of tea without looking at her.

"Hey," she snapped, "what hasn't been? I'm not walking beside you on what's bound to be an all-day trip."

"You're right," he said, glancing up at her. None of the warmth she'd been used to seeing in his eyes was evident. A languid lack of interest was there instead. "We'll take a cab. It's only about a mile out of the park, and a mile back to the little town we passed through just before we got here."

"Hammond. You don't think Mueller might be waiting for us to show up there, knowing they lost us in that vicinity?"

He nodded. "It's possible. That's why we'll go at night, and that's why we'll be very careful."

"I don't have the cash to pay for a cab."

"I do."

"Of course. Dominic Big Shot. Lots of money and a twenty-acre kingdom far away." The remark had begun as sarcasm and ended on a trace of sadness.

The sound made his eyes lose that cool detachment for an instant as they looked into hers. What she saw instead was hot and complex and almost as unsettling as the distance.

"Then, I'm going back to bed," she said. "Wake me when it's..."

When he leapt up and silenced her with a hand over her mouth, she thought for an instant that his cool control had snapped. Then she heard the voices.

With Kellen still pinned against him, his hand to her mouth, Dominic listened. He recognized Mueller's distinctive voice. It was quiet, but authoritative and high for a man. Footsteps were coming toward them down the tunnel.

"Is it him?" Kellen whispered.

He nodded, and pushed her toward the room where they'd slept. "Go get the sleeping bags," he ordered in an undertone, "and bring them here."

As she complied, he swept up everything they'd been using and dropped it into the wood box. Except the little stove, and empty soup can, which he threw out the window, praying the grass was too wet to ignite.

Kellen stumbled in with the bags and he shoved them down the dark well.

"But..." she protested.

"Give me your hand," he ordered.

She did, and he pulled her over the hole until he could place her hand against the first rung of the metal ladder that went down into the darkness. "Feel that?"

"I am not climbing down in there," she whispered adamantly.

"Fine," he replied, "say hi to Mueller for me when he finds you. I'm going down. If you change your mind, follow me."

The voices were growing closer.

"I'm not going down there!" she repeated as Dominic disappeared over the edge and into the darkness.

The voices were just around the bend when she changed her mind, groped for the rung he'd showed her, and stretched a leg into the well, reaching cautiously for another rung somewhere below the first.

She felt a hand close around her ankle and place it on the metal strip.

Approaching footsteps propelled her downward, until she was aware that Dominic had leaned to the side of the ladder and was guiding her down into his arms. He stopped her progress with a hand to her back, then reached for the far end of the rung at her shoulder level, pinning her between him and the concrete tube that enclosed them.

As footsteps rang on the concrete above their heads, Kellen looked up. Dominic put a strong hand to the back of her head and tilted it down, leaning his over her.

She understood then, that with their dark coats and dark hair, they were probably invisible, even to a casual glance over the side.

As footsteps circled the shallow railing, walked the length, then width of the room, then crossed to the window to look out, Kellen felt her heartbeat pound in her ears and her throat. She felt as though she were enclosed in a pressure cooker.

Not only did the firm pressure of Dominic's body against hers render her incapable of movement, but she could feel all its pulse points against her—his temple against her forehead, his heart against her shoulder, his...

She turned that thought off before it could form, because it would make her either scream or moan and now was not the time to do either.

"What makes you think they'd be in here, Mr. Mueller?" a deep, cultured voice asked. "It isn't logical. He's probably hiding out with the hooker."

Kellen's mouth opened, but Dominic quickly put a hand over it.

"It wasn't far from here that we went off the road," another voice said. It was raspy and high-pitched. "I think Mr. Mueller's right. He's still got the hooker with him, so he can't have gotten far."

"Please, Ferguson," a third voice said. "Don't judge all women by *your* wife. Many of them are useful, even valuable."

There was such disdainful cruelty in the sound, Kellen was sure that had to be Mueller.

"And don't presume anything," he went on. "You dealt with him once, remember? He's quick and clever." Footsteps rang on the concrete as someone walked slowly around the railing, then around a second time. "I'd feel better about this if you boys were competent enough to find out who she is."

"We're working on it. Nobody got much of a look at her."

The footsteps stopped directly overhead. Kellen stopped breathing.

"Give me the light, Carter," Mueller ordered.

There was the sound of something changing hands. Kellen felt Dominic free one hand and reach behind him for his gun. She had little difficulty fighting the urge to scream and run. Her heartbeat was choking her and she was suspended in midair in a black hole. She was forced to await her fate in still silence.

"Mr. Mueller!" A fourth voice followed the sound of fresh footsteps into the upstairs room. It was breathless. "Watson's on the cellular. He says he's spotted Hunter's security guy's car in the hospital parking lot in Astoria!"

"All right, let's go. Ferguson, we'll drop you off in Hammond so you can keep a lookout on the chance they've split up and Hunter and the girl show up again."

"Without a car?" Ferguson did not sound pleased.

There was a long-suffering sigh. "Show some initiative. Rent one."

Footsteps died away, and finally the roar of a motor split the silence, then diminished as Mueller and his entourage drove away.

Kellen sagged against the cold metal ladder, relief making her dizzy.

Dominic swatted her lightly on the hip. "Go on up," he said.

Irritation instantly superseded relief. She looked at him over her shoulder. "You know, I'm getting pretty tired of your attitude. And keep your hands to yourself. Old Ferguson might have mistaken me for a hooker, but you know better."

"Could we have this discussion on solid ground?"

"My pleasure!"

Kellen forgot her fear of the pit and the horrid, perpendicular ladder and climbed up, hoisting herself over the top.

Dominic followed, holding her elbow as she stepped over the restraining railing Mueller and his men had leaned over only moments before.

The moment they were on the other side, she yanked out of his grasp and turned on him.

"I may be stuck here with you, but don't think that I have to put up with—"

He took her arms and shook her just enough to silence her. He looked as though his nerves were as frayed as hers felt.

"You will put up with," he told her, keeping his voice down with an effort, "whatever we have to put up with, to get both of us out of this safe and sound."

"I don't—"

He shook her again. "If I can tolerate those sultry looks you give me, your insistence that my home is phony, my parenting poor, my very existence unreal—then have you sleep beside me and climb all over me in your dreams—you can deal with a few inconveniences, too."

Climb all over him in her dreams? So that was why he'd awakened in such an irritable mood. Suddenly and vividly, she recalled a dream that she'd forgotten until this moment.

She and Dominic had been making love in a field of wildflowers, and in the far distance, children played and horses neighed.

Her cheeks flushed scarlet as she looked into his eyes. She saw his eyes note her rise of color and wonder at it.

"I'm sorry." She stiffened. "I'm a restless sleeper. Of course that's no longer a problem now, is it?" She pointed down the black hole. "Our sleeping bags are somewhere down there."

He looked where she pointed, acknowledging that even if he climbed down to get the bags to keep them comfortable until nightfall, they were probably in a puddle of water.

But it wasn't the sleeping bags that constituted the problem, anyway. It was the way he felt everytime he looked at her, and he doubted a solution would present itself anytime soon.

Chapter Seven

"You're sure this is a smart thing to do?" Kellen asked. They stood at the mouth of the tunnel, ready to venture out into the night. It was cold and drizzling, and Kellen felt a longing for her very ordinary but extremely warm and comfortable bed. Fortunately, Dominic left her little time to dwell on it. He was already moving out and pulling her along with him.

"I have to call my kids. And I have to get you somewhere safe. Since they don't know who you are, we should be safe at your place."

"But Mueller told that other guy..."

"Ferguson."

"Ferguson, to wait in Hammond on the chance that we showed up. And that's just what we're going to do?"

"My guess is that Ferguson is already tired of the situation. He's a brilliant attorney married to one of those women who always wants more and more. I think he got into this in the first place to give her what she wants, not to get it for himself. Watch it here. The ground slopes down."

Kellen looked up at him in surprise, then down again, trying to watch her steps in the dark. "How do you know all this about him?"

"By the time I figured out who had really killed Bowles, I pretty much knew who the players were. I was just beginning to learn about them when Mueller came after me."

"But, what does Ferguson waiting for us in Hammond have to do with his greedy wife?"

"Nothing directly. But I could hear the lack of enthusiasm in his voice. He's in this for her, not for himself. He doesn't have the same personal dedication to greed as the others. And he didn't sound thrilled about being left behind. He'll be alone and he'll be careless. We'll be able to flush him out and take him."

That sounded much too easy to Kellen.

"*We'll* be able to flush him out and take him?" she repeated doubtfully. "I decorate windows for a living, remember? I'm not much at hand-to-hand combat."

She saw his grin even in the murky darkness. It had been quick but bright. "No, but you have other compensatory skills. Anyway, you'll flush him out, *I'll* take him. He's all that stands between us, a hot shower, and a comfortable bed."

That was the first time he'd smiled all day. Not that the situation was much to smile about, but he'd had a relatively cheerful attitude about it until that morning. Curiously, his lightening mood made her feel better, too.

They walked at a brisk and steady pace along the winding road out of the state park. It rose and fell for about a mile between tall firs and cedars. The drizzle pattered against the needles and on the leaves of the undergrowth crowded around the base of the trees.

In the woods on both sides, the wind alternately sighed and howled. Kellen found herself holding Dominic's hand tightly and feeling very grateful she wasn't alone.

Before they reached the park gates, the rain turned from a drizzle to a downpour. Dominic opened his coat and wrapped one side of it around Kellen, pulling her close to his side in an effort to protect her from the deluge.

"You're going to get soaked," she protested, trying to push away, but he held her firmly.

"Not if you don't struggle," he said. "Just keep moving."

Just as they reached the entrance to the park, the sound of an automobile approaching on the highway rumbled in the darkness. Dominic pulled Kellen behind the high brick gate and peered around the sign as the pickup truck drove past, windshield wipers beating, headlights picking out the stinging sheets of rain. There was a large black Labrador in the passenger seat.

"We'd better stay off the road," Dominic advised, "and approach that main intersection from the shelter of the trees. My guess is, Ferguson will be somewhere near there."

Kellen frowned worriedly. "But the telephone is across the highway in Corky's parking lot," she said. "Under a light, if I remember correctly. He'll see us."

Dominic nodded. "That's all right. You'll go to the phone booth. I'll watch from cover, and when Ferguson comes for you, I'll come for him."

She was not convinced of the wisdom of the plan. "You're sure he won't just shoot me from wherever he's hiding?"

"Positive," Dominic said confidently. "He only wants you to get to me. He'll think that grabbing you will bring me in."

Rain streamed over both of them as though they stood under a shower. As that thought formed in Kellen's mind, she saw the two of them standing in the tiny shower stall in her bathroom as warm water flowed around them, steam rising like the mystic elements of a dream. It had tightly curled his hair and flushed her cheeks as they stared into each other's eyes, body to body.

Cold rain down her collar snapped her back to the very unromantic present.

"And just when will you arrive on the scene?"

"I don't know," he said with a straight face. "I might wait until he takes you away, then call a cab to take me to the nearest bus station then—who knows? —maybe Mexico."

Indignant, Kellen punched him in the arm. "Very funny."

He caught her small fist and enfolded it in his, his eyes taking on a warning glint despite the rain running down his face.

"I warned you not to hit me again," he said.

She rolled her eyes and stood nose to nose with him, her hair plastered to her head. "You don't scare me,

Hunter. You keep messing with me, and I'll keep hitting you.''

"Messing with you?" he repeated, pinning her to the spot with a look that was at once quelling and challenging. "You consider anything that challenges your complacent view of things is 'messing with you.' I think that's what you're all about, Kellen. You need to be messed with. Only when the time comes, I'm going to go far beyond that. I'm going to turn you right around."

He spoke with complete conviction. It was all she could do to sound disbelieving.

"You think so?"

"I'm absolutely sure of it." He sighed, wondering what in the hell he was doing arguing male-female relationships in a downpour in the middle of the night while Ferguson probably waited for them less than a mile down the road.

Looking up and down the highway and finding both directions free of traffic of any kind, he took Kellen's hand and pulled her with him across the road and into the trees.

The going was sloggy and difficult. The highway sloped down a shallow embankment that caught water and slimy leaves and debris and held it in the trough that ran parallel to the highway.

They moved slowly and carefully, but slipped and slid anyway. Their coats were heavy with mud below the knee by the time they reached what he guessed was Hammond's only four-way intersection.

Still in the shelter of trees, he pulled Kellen in front of him and pointed to the gas station and quick-stop store that took up the southwest corner.

"Is that what you were talking about?"

"Right," she said quietly. "Corky's. See? There's the payphone under the streetlight."

"And there's Ferguson," Dominic said, pointing through the trees to a U-Haul truck parked in the concealing brush. The rain suddenly slowed to a drizzle.

Kellen strained to see where he pointed. The hood of the truck caught the glow of the streetlight, but it was too distant for her to see anyone inside.

"How do you know it's him?"

"What else could he find to rent in a town this size? Most gas stations provide them."

She strained to see, remembering Mueller telling Ferguson to show some initiative and rent a car when he'd protested being left without one. She almost felt sorry for Ferguson, caught between a greedy wife and a ruthless boss, and having to do his furtive best in a U-Haul truck.

She straightened and drew a deep breath. "Okay," she said. "What do you want me to do?"

He frowned down at her. "You're sure you're okay with this?"

She jammed her hands into her coat pockets and found that even the insides were soggy.

"I am," she reassured him, giving him the barest trace of a smile. "But if you take off for Mexico on me, you'd better hire someone to test your margaritas before you drink them because I'm coming after you."

He grinned broadly and pulled her to him for one long, suddenly serious moment. Then he kissed the top of her head and held her away from him.

"Okay. We're going back about a hundred feet, then I want you to run out onto the highway, so that it looks as if you've been following it from the park. And I want you to look over your shoulder as you run, so that he'll think you're trying to get away from me."

She nodded. "So he won't suspect you're hiding in the trees."

"Very good. Now, give it your Sarah Bernhardt best. The more convinced he is that you're alone, the easier it'll be for me to walk right up to him and get him out of our way."

She nodded again, her heart pounding. "Right."

"Ready?"

"Yeah."

"I won't let anything happen to you. I promise."

She wasn't sure why she believed him, but she did. "See you at the phone booth."

Dominic watched her go, keeping pace with her through the trees as she ran along the side of the highway, looking back over her shoulder, the fear on her face stark and convincing. Because it was genuine, he knew.

Fear for her rose inside him. He had no doubt the scenario would enfold as he'd predicted, and that he could easily handle Ferguson. But he also knew the unexpected could leap out at them at any moment.

He waited just inside the shelter of trees bordering Corky's parking lot as Kellen rounded the corner into the broad, glowing triangle under the streetlight.

The telephone booth stood there, every small detail of it outlined in the harsh glow. Everything beyond it receded in the darkness beyond. Dominic strained his eyes to see.

Kellen turned her back to the north side of the street, flipped with all apparent anxiety through the telephone book, then dug a coin out of her purse and made a call.

Dominic saw Ferguson materialize out of the darkness like an apparition. He wore a designer trench coat dotted with raindrops as he skulked across the parking lot, hiding behind cars apparently left for service.

Inside the phone booth, Kellen pretended to carry on an animated conversation, still turned away from Ferguson.

Dominic felt everything inside him tense, begging for the release of action. Ferguson started at a low run toward the phone booth.

Kellen pretended not to hear the footsteps. Her heart was pounding in her ears and her shaking hands clutched the cold telephone so hard she feared she'd break it.

She carried on a fictitious conversation with her mother.

"Mom, you have to come and get me," she cried, the drama and urgency in her voice not entirely planned. Suddenly, the thought of her mother coming to her rescue had a lot of appeal. "I've been kidnapped by this writer, and it's taken me two days to get away from him. I'm in the parking lot at Corky's. What do mean, which corner? How many corners are there in Hammond? Mom, I—"

Suddenly, a hand grabbed her roughly and yanked her just outside the booth. She looked up into a face that wasn't at all what she'd expected. Ferguson was average height, thick in the shoulders but slender, and groomed even at that hour as though he'd just stepped out of a hair salon.

His gray eyes were bleary and ill-tempered, but she didn't find him a frightening figure.

"Put the phone down," he said in a tone he probably intended to be menacing. She thought she might have found it so if she hadn't known Dominic stood just beyond the trees.

"I'm sorry," she said amenably. "You'll have to wait your turn. I'll be through in a minute." She stepped back into the booth and put the receiver to her ear. "Mom, look, someone wants to use the phone. Will you please come and pick me up? I—"

This time he yanked her out of the booth and reached behind her to slam the receiver into place. Out of the corner of her eye, Kellen saw Dominic start at a run across the parking lot. She turned slightly to keep Ferguson's back to him.

"I know who you are," Ferguson said, his beautifully manicured hands biting into her upper arms.

Kellen looked interested. "You do? Who am I?"

"The hooker those goons hired for Hunter," he replied, his expression turning unsettlingly salacious. She felt a cold chill run down her spine. "It's too bad you got away from him just in time to run into me."

Kellen rolled her eyes in pretended exasperation. "Great. I suppose this guy Mueller that Dominic told me about wants me to tell him where he is?"

"He does," Ferguson said. He took Kellen's chin in his hand and leaned over her. She caught a whiff of the salami sandwich he must have eaten while waiting for them to appear.

Kellen's stomach rose up, threatening rebellion, at the same moment that Dominic yanked Ferguson around and delivered one punch to his jaw that knocked him out cold.

"Call a cab!" Dominic ordered quickly, reaching down to rummage in Ferguson's pockets for keys. He sat Ferguson up, slung him over his shoulder and hurried across the street to the U-Haul.

Kellen did as he asked, watching Dominic as she waited for the cab company to pick up. Dominic opened the back of the storage area of the truck and dropped Ferguson in it.

"Coast Cab," a disinterested voice said on the other end of the line.

Kellen gave him their location in as calm a voice as she could muster and hung up. Dominic came running back to her, Ferguson's clothes and shoes balled up in his hands. He threw them into the gas station's Dumpster, then pulled Kellen with him into the shadows under the roof's overhang. "What about the cab?"

"It'll be right here."

"All right. Wait here while I call my kids."

Kellen waited, wet and shivering, as Dominic ran to the phone booth, stabbed out a number, and paced back and forth, watching out the clear sides. He finally hung up and ran back to her. "Line's busy. I'll try again at your place."

The black and yellow cab arrived, cruising slowly, the driver peering out in search of his fare.

He frowned a little nervously at them as they climbed into the back seat. Kellen felt sure he was convinced they were some modern-day Bonnie and

Clyde. Muddy and soaked and probably looking desperate, they must seem like anything but solid citizens.

Dominic slapped him genially on the shoulder. "Glad someone's still up in this town. Our car broke down about a mile back and we couldn't even raise our insurer."

The driver's relieved smile reflected in his rearview mirror. "Makes you wonder what you pay the big premiums for, doesn't it? Where do you want to go? Red Lion Inn?"

"No, we're going to Sandpiper to stay with friends. Give him the address, honey."

Fascinated with his easy and thoroughly convincing performance, Kellen required a moment to realize she was "honey." She told the driver her address, then gave Dominic a glance of disapproval.

He pulled her into his arm and leaned back, expelling a long sigh. She leaned against him, partly because the driver, watching them in the mirror, would expect her to, and partly because she was exhausted and giddy with relief at the knowledge that she'd be home in fifteen minutes.

"Looks like nobody's up," the driver remarked as he pulled up in front of the simple frame cottage with its peaked roof and deep front porch. "Left the porch light on for you, though."

Dominic paid and tipped the driver, then followed Kellen up the steps. As she unlocked the door, he looked around for any sign that their arrival was being noticed.

But up and down the street that fronted the broad beach, there was not a light on anywhere. The row of unpretentious little cottages was quiet and dark.

Kellen pushed her way in, flipped on a light, then stood aside to let Dominic follow her. She closed and locked the door as he looked around at her mismatched collection of flower-patterned sofa, two threadbare mission-style chairs, a glass-topped wicker coffee table, and plank and concrete-block bookcases.

From out of the shadows across the living room, a blur of orange ran at them.

"Carrot!" Kellen clapped her hands and a fat orange cat leapt into her arms, purring loud enough to rattle windows. "My poor baby," she cooed at the cat as she stroked and scratched and rubbed her chin against the feline's face. "Good thing you have a self-feeder, isn't it?"

Dominic reached over to stroke a knuckle over the cat's head. Carrot leaned over to make it easy for him, baring her teeth in ecstasy rather than anger, and rubbing a formidable incisor against his hand.

"Looks like the cat missed you," Dominic said.

Kellen gave him a teasing glance. "She thinks I'm *fun* to have around. Sit down."

"God, this looks comfortable," he groaned, gazing longingly down at the sofa. "But I don't dare touch anything until I've had a shower. Before I do that, though, can I use your phone?" He looked at his watch. It was one-thirty a.m. It would be two-thirty where his boys were. Too early to call if everything was all right, but already too late if everything wasn't. He had to know.

Kellen brought him a portable telephone, took his coat, and pushed him onto the sofa. "Get comfortable. I'll make some coffee."

The annoying buzz of a busy signal frustrated him. He prowled in the direction Kellen had taken and found her in a large, square, yellow and white kitchen that seemed to be doing double duty as a warehouse. One half of it was stacked with boxes. Wedged into a corner was a desk littered with papers. Carrot sat in the middle of them, contentedly grooming herself.

At the counter on the other side of the room, Kellen ground coffee beans. The aroma of rich, faintly sweet smelling coffee teased his nostrils.

"Irish Creme is my favorite," she said, glancing at him over her shoulder as he approached. "I hope you like it. It's all I have around."

"Smells wonderful. Two days on pop and tea was almost as bad as having our lives in danger."

"Did you get through to your uncle?"

"Line was busy." He punched the number out and tried again, frowning at the buzz of the busy signal.

"Still busy. Can I do anything?"

"Would you like a sandwich?" She crossed to the refrigerator and held the door open, examining the contents.

It was tidy, he noticed over her shoulder, not very full, but tidy.

"I'd offer you an omelette," she said, turning to give him a teasing smile, "but your omelette intimidated me. I couldn't—" She stopped midsentence when she found her mouth a mere two inches from his. She was afraid to move it, afraid to draw in a breath, afraid to lose the slender thread of control that had been fraying steadily since she'd walked into the house.

There was something about being in her cozy surroundings that made all the threats he represented seem somehow less dangerous—even appealing. She liked the sight of him among her things, big and mysterious and still maintaining that princely storybook air. Right here in her kitchen, he truly did seem like a fantasy come to life.

She lost her train of thought.

He turned her around, pushed the refrigerator door closed and took her into his arms.

He should be keeping his mind on the danger, Dominic told himself. He should remain alert. But if he didn't indulge himself for one moment, he was going to slip over the edge. And she always seemed to restore him. A kiss from her was like life support. And they were safe for the time being.

He could see in her mossy green eyes that she wanted this as much as he did. She was afraid of it, too, but he understood that. He thought again how well she'd behaved in a situation that should have scared her senseless.

She'd been kidnapped and brought to him, a perfect stranger, been holed up in a damp, dark tunnel, dragged—soaking wet—two miles in the middle of the night, then used as bait to catch a murdering thief. And still, she was looking at him with desire in her eyes, waiting for him to kiss her.

He framed her face in his hands. "Pretend," he said softly, "that we just met tonight—at a party. That we talked a little, danced a little, and I've brought you home."

She shook her head and looped her arms around his neck. "Meeting at a party is so conventional. I kind of like the way we met. The whole thing became very..." she considered the right word "...dramatic, I guess. The stuff legends are made of."

A frown pinched between his eyebrows. "But that makes you think what we feel for each other isn't real."

She kissed his chin. "We don't have to worry about what's real and what isn't until this is over. Right now, this time is something special. Separate. Just ours. A few days out of our lives that don't have to be analyzed or lived according to anyone's code."

Her analysis of the situation wasn't completely satisfying, but the passion in her eyes was. The day would come when he'd have to deal with their differing attitudes on the future. But she was right about this time—here in her beachfront cottage. This was all theirs.

He cupped her head in his hand and kissed her, doing his best to erase everything that existed beyond their charmed little sphere. He kissed her tenderly, in appreciation for how easy she'd made the last few days for him, considering how any other woman might have reacted. Then he kissed her hotly, greedily, in gratitude for having introduced an element into his life that would never let it be easy again.

He was back in the fray, he knew. The battle of the sexes had another pair of sparring partners.

Then he stroked down her back, over her hip, then up again just to give her pleasure, and to please himself. He felt little tremors of response under his hands and wished his brain was free to pursue this further.

AN IMPORTANT MESSAGE
FROM
THE EDITORS OF HARLEQUIN®

Dear Reader,

Because you've chosen to read one of our fine romance novels, we'd like to say "thank you"! And, as a **special** way to thank you, we've selected <u>four more</u> of the <u>books</u> you love so well, **and** a Victorian Picture Frame to send you absolutely *FREE!*

Please enjoy them with our compliments...

Editor,
American Romance

Debra Matteucci

P.S. And <u>because</u> we value our customers, we've attached something extra inside ...

EDITOR'S
FREE
GIFT
SEAL
THANK YOU

PEEL OFF SEAL AND
PLACE INSIDE

HOW TO VALIDATE
YOUR
EDITOR'S FREE GIFT
"THANK YOU"

1. Peel off gift seal from front cover. Place it in space provided at right. This automatically entitles you to receive four free books and a lovely pewter-finish Victorian Picture Frame.

2. Send back this card and you'll get brand-new Harlequin American Romance® novels. These books have a cover price of $3.50 each, but they are yours to keep absolutely free.

3. There's no catch. You're under no obligation to buy anything. We charge nothing—ZERO—for your first shipment. And you don't have to make any minimum number of purchases—not even one!

4. The fact is thousands of readers enjoy receiving books by mail from the Harlequin Reader Service®. They like the convenience of home delivery...they like getting the best new novels months before they're available in stores...and they love our discount prices!

5. We hope that after receiving your free books you'll want to remain a subscriber. But the choice is yours—to continue or cancel, anytime at all! So why not take us up on our invitation, with no risk of any kind. You'll be glad you did!

6. Don't forget to detach your FREE BOOKMARK. And remember...just for validating your Editor's Free Gift Offer, we'll send you FIVE MORE gifts, *ABSOLUTELY FREE!*

YOURS FREE!
*This lovely Victorian pewter-finish miniature is perfect for displaying a treasured photograph—and it's yours **absolutely free**—when you accept our no-risk offer!*

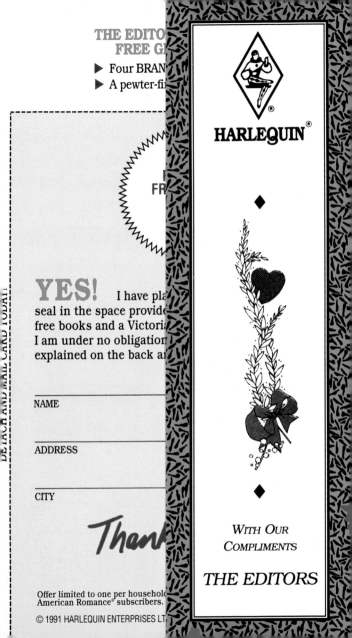

HARLEQUIN®

WITH OUR
COMPLIMENTS

THE EDITORS

As much as he wanted that, his thoughts were divided. He couldn't sway his mind from concern for his children.

Kellen felt everything inside her come to life, despite her exhaustion. As his hands wandered over her, those places he hadn't touched seemed to tense in anticipation. She felt the tick of every pulse in her body, the beat of her heart, the ebb and flow of air in her lungs.

Then he rested his forehead against hers for an instant, and drew in a steadying breath. The retreat of his hands was like the loss of an extra sense. His touch had allowed her to read him as well as herself, and her body suddenly didn't seem whole without that ability.

He raised his head and pinched her chin between his thumb and forefinger.

"I have to call my children again," he said.

"Of course. I'll nuke some leftovers."

Dominic walked restlessly around the room as he jabbed the redial on the portable phone. He felt enormous relief when the line rang.

Until Rocco answered. Then he heard the tension in his uncle's voice immediately.

"Hello? Yes?" There was an expectant sound to the words, as though something wasn't right, and he was hoping this call would make it so.

"Unc, it's Dom," he said, fighting an instant upsurge of fear and adrenaline. "What's the matter?"

"What's the matter? What's the matter!" Rocco replied at full voice, so that Dominic had to move the receiver away from his ear. When Rocco shouted, it usually indicated that he'd lost control in some way.

"Where the hell are you? I've been worried sick! Nobody's checked in for two days!"

Spike hadn't checked in. Not a good sign.

"I'm fine," Dominic replied. "We had a few problems. Gordy and Spike . . . well, we got separated."

"Separated? I told them not to leave you for a minute."

"They didn't do it willingly. I'm not sure where they are, but the safe house was compromised, we couldn't raise Burton's men, so we all split up."

There was cursing on the other end of the line.

"Uncle, I just wanted to be sure the boys are all right."

It was barely a heartbeat's hesitation, but Dominic heard it.

"I'm sure they're fine . . ." Rocco said quickly.

Dominic felt his blood freeze and stall his heart. "Rocco, what is it?"

"Well, they're . . . missing."

Dread swept down Dominic's body from his scalp to the soles of his feet. No. No. He wouldn't let it be. He was vaguely aware of Kellen turned from the counter, a spreading tool in her hands, her eyes wide.

"You mean," he made himself ask, "they've been taken?"

"No, damn it!" Rocco said, his voice rising again. "I mean they're missing. Took a powder. Ran away!"

Dominic didn't know whether to feel relief or heightened fear. Ran away? A fourteen-year-old and a nine-year-old. Alone. With eight hundred miles separating them from their father.

"We were having lunch and Paddy came in to tell me it was way past checking-in time and we hadn't heard from Gordy or Spike. I tried to tell the boys not to worry, that it didn't necessarily mean trouble, but when the next check-in time passed without word from you, I went to their room to tell them I was sending a couple of men out to find out what the hell was going on. They had rolled up their sleeping bags in their beds to make it look like they were there but, hey, I ain't stupid! But don't worry. I got men out looking. I'm sure they think they're coming to your rescue, but how far can they get?''

Dominic tried to make his brain function despite the panic that wanted to seize it. The second check-in time. They'd been missing more than thirty-six hours.

"But they don't know where I am," he said.

Rocco's voice lowered. "Well, they might. They could have overheard me giving my men instructions. But don't worry, I've got men looking for them," Rocco went on in a placating tone. "They probably went to the highway and tried to hitch a ride."

His boys were hitchhiking? God!

"Where the hell are you?" Rocco demanded suddenly.

"At a friend's," Dominic replied, walking across the kitchen to grab the coat Kellen had thrown with hers over the back of a chair.

"What friend? You don't know anybody out there."

"A woman."

"What woman?" The concern grew in Rocco's voice. "Dom, what the hell is going on out there?"

"Look, Roc, I've got to go. The boys are undoubtedly coming this way. I've got to get to the safe house before they do or Mueller might get them."

"Dom, I found Mrs. Bowles. She's going to talk."

At that moment, what should have been good news meant very little.

"Dom!" Rocco shouted. "My men are on the way. You stay put! You hear me?"

Dominic hit the off button and slapped the antenna down.

"What's happened?" Kellen asked, shrugging into her own coat.

Briefly, he related his conversation with Rocco. "Can you call me a cab?"

She handed him a commuter mug of coffee. "You're a cab. Come with me."

"Fine time to be funny. And where do you think you're going?"

She led him out the back door of the kitchen, snatched a set of keys off a hook near the door and flipped on a light that revealed a concrete pad with a basketball hoop—and an ancient green Ford truck parked under it.

"Second car," she said. "And it doesn't respond to anyone but me. Hop in."

Dominic caught her arm and stopped her in the pool of glaring light. "No," he declared firmly. "You're not coming. Give me the keys."

She put them behind her back. "I drive, or I'll call you a cab. The first way, we're out of here in twenty seconds, the second, you wait ten, maybe fifteen min—"

With a look that said they'd settle up later, Dominic walked around the truck and climbed in.

Chapter Eight

The safe house and the three acres that surrounded it were dark as pitch. Dominic and Kellen lay on their stomachs in the wet grass that covered the slope behind the house. They'd left her asthmatic truck a quarter of a mile back down the road, and Kellen had led him in over an old log bridge that crossed the creek and allowed them to approach unseen. Mercifully, the rain had stopped. "Do you think Mueller is here?"

Dominic shook his head. "But he's probably having it watched."

Kellen said urgently, "Dominic, what if your boys show up and think you're still in the house? They'll walk right up..."

Dominic felt as though an anvil lay in the pit of his stomach. That thought had occurred to him, too, but he'd calmed himself with a reminder of how intelligent and resourceful his boys were. Those very qualities in them had aged him considerably in the last few years, but he was confident they would stand them in good stead when they arrived.

"They took off because they knew there was a problem here," he said, praying he was right about this. "They'll move carefully when they get here. Besides, if they're hitching, they might not even get here until daylight."

Dominic considered the down side of the slope and the high hedge between it and the house, then turned to Kellen.

"I want you to stay here," he said softly. "I'm going closer to see what we're up against. Whistle if you see any sign of the boys, or if someone comes out of the house."

Kellen caught his arm as he started down the slope. "I can't whistle."

"Then just clap your hands."

He saw her roll her eyes as the clouds parted to reveal a watery moon. "Sure. Like they're going to believe a bird is sitting up here clapping its hands."

There were times when he wondered if she and his boys had somehow attended the same training program to drive him crazy.

"Forget the whole thing," he said. "I'll take my chances." Then he pushed her back down to the grass. "They won't be looking for anyone coming from the creek side, but stay down anyway."

Kellen watched, impotent with frustration, as he disappeared down the shadowy slope of the hill.

He crouched for a moment, then ran to the base of a wide maple halfway to the hedge.

Kellen strained to keep her eye on him. Then she blinked, wondering if she was really seeing what she thought she was seeing, or if fear was causing her to hallucinate.

Something slipped slowly out of the umbrella of bare twigs and branches, then eased itself down toward Dominic. When it struck him in the head, and she heard the muffled thud of contact, she left her hiding spot and ran down the slope, slipping in her haste, regaining her footing, then running for all she was worth. She launched herself at the pair still struggling as Dominic tried to stand.

Dominic felt a second projectile strike him and his first attacker. The impact took all three of them to the ground. As he felt wet grass invade his ears, his hair, his collar, he turned all his energies to repelling the attack.

And that's when he became aware that there was something strange about it. He caught a fist before it connected with his face and diverted it far more easily than he should have been able to had it been another man. Also, he was aware that Kellen had entered the melee, and she and his opponent struggled together on the battlefield of his chest.

He heard a very familiar grunt just as a third projectile hit them and dragged Kellen off of him.

His first opponent, free of Kellen, drew his fist back again. Dominic grabbed the puny arm attached to it and yanked the slim body down to him.

"Ethan, it's me!" he whispered.

The struggle stopped. Even Kellen, dealing with the most recent participant, looked up from astride him.

Ethan peered closer, then sat back, eyes wide. "Holy cow!"

The sound of feet moving in the grass came from the other side of the hedge.

Considering it fortunate their struggle hadn't taken them far from the tree, Dominic yanked Ethan down beside him and lay absolutely still. Beside him, Kellen lay half-atop Travis, her hand over his mouth. In a fragile wedge of moonlight, two men appeared with submachine guns to look over the chest-high hedge.

"You're just nervous," one of the men said after a moment. "It's probably just racoons."

"Racoons don't speak words," the other man retorted, his tone indignant.

There was soft laughter. "How do you know? We don't get that many of them in Boston on the fourteenth floor of the Mueller Building."

"Very funny."

"Come on back. There's nothing there."

The moment the door closed, the boys were all over Dominic. Kellen watched, a lump in her throat, as they hugged silently but effusively.

Then Dominic was on his feet, shepherding the boys and Kellen up the slope to the road. He led them at a quick pace the full quarter mile to the truck, everything about him emanating anger.

Kellen hung behind as he pushed both boys up into the passenger side of the bench seat and glowered up at them with paternal censure.

"What in the hell are you doing here?" he demanded quietly.

"We came to rescue you!" Travis, sitting farther inside, leaned around his older brother with a broad grin.

He had sandy blond hair, Kellen saw in the truck's interior light, and pale blue eyes. Despite his father's apparent anger, he was obviously delighted to have found him. He was probably as single-minded as his father, she thought, remembering with a private smile, the fight he'd put up against her on the lawn.

Ethan gave Travis an impatient look, then turned back to his father, his expression and his attitude slightly belligerent.

He looked just like his father, Kellen noted. Dark hair, dark eyes, and the suggestion of strong features that would mature into dangerous good looks.

"We overheard Uncle Rocco talking with one of his men," he explained. "They said there was trouble at the safe house."

Dominic nodded tightly. "And it never occurred to you that trained adults could handle the problem more easily than you could? Or that you'd scare everyone to death by disappearing?"

Ethan's eyes brimmed dangerously. "All I thought about was that when Mom was in trouble, we couldn't do anything about it because it was a disease. Now you were in trouble, but it was just men and guns. We could fight that."

"Yeah!" Travis chimed in.

"So, after all my lectures about hitchhiking," Dominic said, the emotion in his voice belying the anger in his eyes, "you just take off—"

Travis leaned around his brother again. "We didn't hitchhike, Dad. Honest."

Dominic frowned from one boy to the other. "Then how did you get here?"

Travis beamed, apparently certain they were in for praise. "We stole a car!"

Dominic let his forehead thunk against the top of the doorframe. Barely suppressing the laughter bubbling up inside her, Kellen walked around the truck and got in behind the wheel.

"You guys are going to make me an old man before my time," Dominic muttered, pulling Travis out from the middle, slipping in beside Ethan and setting the younger boy in his lap.

Travis frowned at him, an elbow resting on Dominic's shoulder as the boy reclined against him. "You're already old, aren't you?"

Dominic put an arm around Ethan's shoulders, finally letting relief and tenderness supersede the tension and anger.

"And getting older all the time. You all right?" he asked Ethan.

The boy leaned against him for several seconds, then straightened and drew a deep breath. "Yeah. Glad we found you, though. It was starting to get scary."

"Where did you leave this car?"

"A ways back," Ethan replied. "Just like you did. We didn't want them to hear us coming up."

Kellen glanced at Dominic over the boy's head. He raised an eyebrow, trying to suppress pride as his eyes said I-told-you-so. He had known they'd be careful.

"Ah...Dad?" Ethan hooked his thumb in Kellen's direction. "Aren't you going to introduce us to your chauffeur?"

"Sorry. Of course. Kellen, this is Ethan and Travis. Guys, this is my...friend, Kellen."

Astutely, both boys noticed the pause.

"Friend?" Ethan questioned with a very man-to-man look.

"Is she your lover?" Travis asked candidly.

"Oh, God," Ethan said, putting a hand over his face.

Dominic simply closed his eyes and sighed.

"I said she was my *friend,*" he repeated patiently. "And what do you know about lovers anyway?"

"Not much," Travis said. He leaned back against his father and Dominic was about to breathe a sigh of relief when he added, "Except that you sleep with them. And sometimes you have babies."

RAIN BEGAN TO FALL in earnest again as Kellen pulled the truck around the back of the house.

"Are you two hungry?" she asked as she led the way through the kitchen. Carrot ran up to greet them. Travis picked him up and rubbed his face in the cat's fur.

"Yeah!" Travis said heartily. "We had hamburgers the first day, but yesterday and today all we ate was Doritos and Pepsi. What's his name?"

As Dominic went into the living room with the portable phone, Kellen opened the refrigerator door. "Her name's Carrot." Two very interested onlookers peered over her shoulder.

Ethan rubbed his lean stomach. "You don't have any *real* carrots in there, do you?"

"I do. And some leftover spaghetti."

Their reaction was not only favorable but enthusiastic. In ten minutes she had the spaghetti warmed in the microwave, bread and butter on the table, and raw vegetables on a plate with a dollop of salad dressing in the middle.

She wondered about the wisdom of such a heavy meal at that hour of the morning, then decided it didn't matter. They'd been up all night, and she had no idea what this day would bring. They may as well face it on full stomachs.

Dominic came back into the kitchen, sniffing the air. "Do I smell spaghetti?" he asked in disbelief, going to stand over his younger son.

Travis rolled a bite on his fork and offered it up to his father. Dominic shook his head and reached past the boy for a carrot stick.

"This is delicious," Ethan said, winking at his father as he drew in a long noodle. "She fits Requirement Number Four."

"Spaghetti's Number Three," Travis corrected. "Peanut butter fudge was Number Four."

Kellen looked away from pouring milk to stare at Dominic in confusion.

"The Hunter Family Rules for the Fairy Stepmother," he explained, clutching the carrot stick in his teeth like a cheroot as he came to take the two glasses of milk from her and carry them to the table.

"Fairy Stepmother," she repeated.

Dominic nodded, then bit the end off the carrot stick as he came back to the counter to join her. "She works magic, but she doesn't disappear."

"I see. And how many rules are there?"

Dominic turned to the boys with a questioning look.

"Eight," Ethan replied.

"Nine," Travis corrected. "You forgot we just added the singing one."

Ethan looked first sheepish, then slightly defensive. "Yeah, but that was only because it was dark and we were scared. That's probably not a fair one."

"We didn't say she had to be a *good* singer," Travis argued. "Just that she *would* sing."

Dominic moved the step stool from the edge of the counter to the small two-person table around which the boys sat.

"When were you scared?" he asked quietly.

"I was scared all the time," Travis replied candidly. Then he looked at Ethan with respect. "But Ethan didn't get scared 'til last night in the woods."

"The woods?"

Ethan toyed with his spaghetti, rolling it onto his fork, then letting it fall off again. "We slept in the car, and I was afraid if we did that on the road, a state policeman would come and check us out or something. So I pulled off onto this logging road."

"And what happened?"

"Nothing." Ethan shrugged a shoulder. "It was just dark and quiet and...I was wishing you were with us."

"Or that Mom was," Travis added, looking up from his glass with a milk mustache. "We started talking about the time the axel broke on the station wagon in Texas and you had to hitch a ride to the nearest town and Mom sang to us until you got back."

"You were only four," Dominic said gently. "You remember that?"

As Travis nodded emphatically, Ethan amended, "I don't know if he really remembers it, or thinks he does because I've told him the story so many times."

"Whatever the reason, it's good to have good memories for times when you're scared." He put a hand on Ethan's arm. "And I appreciate you guys coming to my rescue. I really do. Even though you scared me to death and almost knocked me out cold."

Both boys started to laugh. "You're not going to ground us for that, are you?" Travis asked. "We didn't know it was you. We thought you were one of Mueller's men, and Kellen, too."

"No, I can forgive that," Dominic told them. "You have to work out your own deal with Kellen, though. Incidentally, what did you guys do for gas for the car on the road?"

The boys exchanged a quick, guilty look. Dominic had a feeling he was going to wish he hadn't asked.

"What?"

"We used the credit card," Ethan answered, staring at his spaghetti.

"What credit card?"

Ethan looked up at him, his expression one of reluctant resignation. "The one that was in the glove compartment. I think it was a company thing, or something. They never asked us any questions."

Oh, good, Dominic thought. Automobile theft *and* credit card fraud.

He studied his older son closely. He had a strong jaw already, and the early signs of good, firm features, but he would never pass for eighteen. Still, he had.

"I can't believe no one ever questioned you."

Travis laughed. "That's because he had a plan."

Another loaded question.

"What plan?"

"He put a cigarette in his mouth and turned the radio up really high. He looked older, and the gas pump guys were anxious to get rid of us."

Dominic shook his head, torn between pride and horror.

Ethan measured his father's expression and grimaced. "I'm in a lot of trouble, aren't I?"

Dominic considered him another moment, and finally shook his head again. "Not with me. You were very brave and very resourceful. When it's all over and we have an opportunity to explain and pay for the car and the charges on the card, everyone will be happy."

Ethan looked visibly relieved.

"He thought he was going to have to go to jail," Travis said, his plate cleared, his glass empty. "And me, too, cause I was his accomplished."

"Accomplice," Ethan corrected with a glance across the table at his brother. It held the complete exasperation of sibling responsibility, but a grudging affection, too.

"I hate to admit it," he said to Dominic, "but he was a pretty good accomplice. At one place where we stopped for gas and to buy a pop, the guy looked at us like he thought something wasn't right. There was a police car getting gas behind us and I think he was going to go talk to him about us, but Travis pretended he had to barf. The guy gave him some water, washed his face, and by the time we got back to the pump, the cop was gone. The guy just filled us up and let us go."

Dominic frowned, though there was laughter in his eyes. "Promise me you won't go into this stuff professionally, okay? I mean, I'm glad you were clever enough to find me, but I'd hate to think you were too good at theft and joyriding."

Travis shook his head, his eyes growing heavy lidded. "I just want to go home. I'd even like to go back to school."

"How about a shower and a comfortable bed to sleep in?" Kellen suggested.

"The bed sounds good," Travis admitted.

Kellen pulled out his chair. "Come on with me. I'll show you where everything is."

Travis turned back to Dominic uncertainly. "You're staying, aren't you?"

Puzzled by the question, Dominic nodded. "Yeah. Why?"

"Well, you said she wasn't your lover," he replied. "But you're sleeping here. That's weird, isn't it?"

Ethan groaned. "God, you're stupid. This is an emergency, remember? We stole a car. We don't do that every day, but there was no other way to get to Dad, so we did it. It's the same with Dad and Kellen. They're sleeping in the same house 'cause it's an emergency." He turned to his father in disgust. "How come you had a kid that's so dumb?"

"I'm not dumb!" Travis said defensively, taking a threatening step toward his brother. Dominic stood to stop him with a hand on his bony shoulder. Travis subsided wearily, sighing. "I just...don't get all this stuff." He looked up at Kellen. "I'm sorry."

"Hey, don't apologize to me," she said, grinning at Dominic over her shoulder as she led Travis toward the bathroom. "I don't understand this stuff any better than you do."

As Kellen and Travis disappeared into a corridor off the kitchen, Dominic began to clear the table. Ethan rose to help him, keeping his back to him as he shuttled plates back and forth, carefully avoiding his eyes.

Dominic saw the problem, had recognized it in the outburst at the table over Travis's bold but innocent question.

He finally stopped him with a hand on his shoulder and turned him around. Tears were spilling from his eyes and his face crumpled as Dominic pulled him into his arms.

"I was so afraid you were dead," he wept against Dominic's shoulder. "I was so afraid it was going to be just me and Travis. I'm not ready to be in charge. I was scared to death the whole time."

Dominic held him close, his throat constricted with emotion. It was something to know his sons loved him. But it was something else again to know what they'd put themselves through—Ethan particularly—in demonstrating it. And though the boy had grown a good four inches in the past year, he still felt childlike in his arms.

"Well, you don't have to worry about that because I intend to be around for a good long time," he said finally. "But let me tell you that if you had to wait to feel ready or to feel fearless before you could be put in charge of anything, we'd have a world in chaos. No one would ever lead anyone or anything anywhere." He pushed him slightly away from him to look into his eyes. Usually, he saw only himself there, but this morning there was that sweet, vulnerable trace of his wife. "Let me assure you that you did very well getting here. Whether or not it was right to leave is another issue. You decided on what you had to do and you did it very well. You kept your brother and yourself safe." He laughed lightly. "You didn't even wreck the car."

Ethan swiped a hand across his eyes and nodded, apparently anxious to accept his assessment of the situation.

"Driving was easy. I've sat beside you while you were driving for so long that I just knew what to do. But I'm sure glad you're still in charge. I did what I thought were the right things to do about finding you and taking care of Travis, but I never really knew for sure. That's a weird feeling."

Dominic nodded. Ethan had learned a lesson no amount of lecturing on his part could have taught. "Welcome to adulthood." He put an arm around his shoulder and led him toward the sounds of Kellen laughing with Travis. "Only you can ease into it until you're ready for full involvement."

"It's been a long time since I told you this," Ethan said, lowering his voice as they approached the bedroom. "But, I love you, Dad."

Dominic turned to hold him again, his heart full. "I love you, too, Son. And everything's going to be all right. I swear."

"Yeah, I know," Ethan replied with the complete confidence of a boy who'd relinquished control of the situation back to his father.

Travis wore an old football jersey nightshirt Kellen had unearthed. He knelt in the middle of the bed, laughing at the antics of Carrot, who carried on a life-and-death struggle with a chair leg, seemingly unmindful of the fact that it wasn't putting up much of a fight.

Travis looked up at Ethan, his scrubbed and shiny face split in a wide grin. "Rule Number Two," he said, pointing to the cat.

Ethan smiled and nodded.

Kellen, guessing the boys referred to the mother search rules, rose off the corner of the bed, pressing a pair of gray sweatpants and an old T-shirt into Ethan's hands.

"Best I could do," she said.

Ethan shook open the T-shirt. There was a large red rose on it. He looked around the room at his companions, his expression lethal.

"Anyone who opens his mouth to any of my friends—dies."

"Got it."

"Right."

"Absolutely."

"Bathroom's in there." Kellen pointed. "Just holler if you need anything before you go to bed."

Dominic remained to pull the blankets over Travis. The shower pounded beyond the bathroom door, and from the kitchen came the sounds of Kellen rinsing dishes and filling the dishwasher.

Travis wrapped his arms around Dominic's neck and held him crushingly close for a long moment. "I'm glad you're okay, Dad." Then he released him, still grinning. "And I think it's cool that you like Kellen. She fits Rule Number Two, too. She likes animals."

Dominic perched on the edge of the bed beside him. "Ethan explained this, remember? It's an emergency."

Travis dug his elbow into his pillow and rested his cheek on his hand. His grin never wavered. "That's not the whole thing, though. I can tell. You'd like her even if it wasn't an emergency."

There was no reason to evade. "I would. She's quite a lady."

"She thinks you're neat, too."

He found himself greedy for more information. "She does?" he asked casually.

"She said . . ." Travis took on a grave expression as he repeated, "'Your father's a very special man, Travis. Of course I'm fond of him.'"

Dominic winced. "You *asked* her that?"

Travis fell onto his back, frowning. "Sure. You're always saying you'll find answers to all your questions on the tip of your tongue. Ask."

Dominic groaned. How did he explain that the rules that applied in male-female relationships were not necessarily the common sense rules that applied in life.

Travis turned onto his elbow. "Is fond the same as love?"

"Well . . ." Truth to tell, he found "fond" a very unsatisfying word. "It's a gentler form of it."

"Hmm." Travis's eyebrows beetled over that. "But love that makes people get married isn't supposed to be like that, is it? I mean, it's supposed to be hot, passionate stuff."

Dominic kept a straight face. He wasn't sure what emotion he'd have expressed anyway—amusement or chagrin.

"Passionate?"

"Yeah, you know. It makes you need to run laps, or take a cold shower, or go to bed all the time and do—"

"I know what passionate means," Dominic interrupted quickly. "I didn't know you did."

"Oh, sure. Ethan told me that first night when we couldn't sleep. We were talking about Mom, then Mom and you and how we were born and stuff. And I just thought...you probably miss that if it's supposed to be so great.''

Dominic imagined himself one day coming face-to-face with St. Peter and being flung into the far recesses of the darkness reserved for bad parents. Not only had his children stolen a car and used someone else's credit card for eight hundred miles, but his fourteen-year-old had spent the long nights explaining to his little brother with apparently considerable detail the fine points of sex.

''Anyway...'' Travis went on. ''I don't think fond's going to be good enough for Rule Number One.''

''What is Rule Number One?'' Dominic asked, hoping to catch the child off guard. So far, that rule had remained a secret between his boys.

''Can't tell ya,'' Travis replied with no visible remorse. ''But it's the most important one.'' His sudden yawn was huge and lengthy. ''Good night.''

''Good night.'' Dominic leaned down to kiss him and tuck in the blankets.

Ethan emerged from the bathroom in the sweats that climbed to midcalf on him, and the T-shirt with the photographic rose dead center.

Dominic saw an air about him that startled him into a new realization.

''I was looking in the mirror,'' Ethan said, ''and the rose doesn't look so bad. I mean, I'd never buy it, but I thought it'd make me look really stupid, and it's not so bad.'' He frowned as he caught another glimpse of himself in the mirror over the dresser. ''What do you suppose that means?''

Dominic clapped him on the shoulder. ''That you're man enough to carry it off. Good night.''

As Dominic pulled the door closed behind him, he heard Travis say sleepily, "You look stupid even with*out* the rose."

"Go to sleep, feet breath."

Dominic felt something ease inside him. They were all still in danger, but they were together—and things had taken one step back to normal.

He headed resolutely toward the living room where he could see Kellen unfolding a Hide-a-bed. There was another step he'd been intending to take for most of the last forty-eight hours.

Chapter Nine

"What do you mean, you're 'fond' of me?" Dominic demanded, turning Kellen around, pushing her onto the mattress over which she'd pulled only half the sheet, and pinning her there.

"Dominic!" Kellen whispered. "The boys!"

"They'll be asleep in seconds," he predicted knowledgeably. "And don't change the subject. What the hell kind of a word is 'fond'?"

In her vulnerable position, her arms pinned to her sides, Kellen counted on hauteur to help her maintain distance. And she had to. She'd just seen the kind of tight relationship Dominic had with his boys, she'd heard them talk about how thoughts of their mother had gotten them through a frightening time, and concluded there wasn't room for her in their midst—even if this *was* real.

"It means I like you," she responded, keeping all sign of the love she'd begun to feel, the desire that always simmered inside her, under a tight lid. "It means I have affection for you."

"Affection." He repeated the word as though he didn't believe it. "You feel a hell of a lot more for me than affection."

She rolled her eyes as though tired of the subject and of him. "Well, if you know everything, why are you asking me?"

"Because I want you to admit it before I make love to you," he said, his fingers inching up under her sweater. "I want you to look into my eyes and admit that you love me."

She averted her eyes, knowing everything she felt was there. She pretended a bored perusal of the wall behind his shoulder. "I do not love you," she stated.

He inched the sweater up a little more and leaned down to plant a kiss on the silky stripe of exposed flesh at her waist. He felt a nerve kick under his lips.

Determined to ignore him, certain her detachment would make him stop, Kellen closed her eyes and struggled for control. But she'd dreamed about his lips exploring her body; the effort separated her control from her will and made the struggle more than difficult.

And his soft, dry mouth was planting soft kisses up the little incline formed by her rib cage. Feeling, reaction, response fought to work its way to the surface, but she resolutely suppressed it.

"Then why..." he asked, now kneeling astride her, "are you still with me?"

He nudged the sweater up over her lace-covered breasts and paused to kiss the gentle swell of one, and then the other.

She was certain he felt the clamor inside her. Emotions surging within her made her heart beat out of control.

"You prevented me..." She forced the words up through the chaos of her consciousness. "...from leaving."

The sweater was now off. Eyes still closed, she felt the coolness of the room against her skin, felt goose bumps rise as he ran his hands lightly up her arms, over her shoulders, then down again, stopping to rest each hand along the side of a breast. Sensation effervesced along her skin and started a dangerous little thrum at the heart of her femininity.

"Why did you come with me to wait for the boys?" he asked softly. He swept both hands over her ribs and waist to the waistband of her old corduroy pants. He unbuttoned them and began to inch the zipper down.

She had to stop him. Now. She pushed him off her easily and sat up. Too easily, she thought with suspicion.

He sat up beside her, reaching around her to unfasten her bra. She put both hands on his arms to stop him. He merely leaned forward to nibble at the tense cord in her neck.

"Because... because they were children," she said, having to split her concentration from the delicious little shudders he was causing inside her to the words she was trying to speak in a convincing fashion. But even to her own ears they sounded small and untrue. "What woman," she added, hoping to firm them up, "wouldn't be...wouldn't be...concerned for the safety of...children?"

He raised his head to look into her eyes. His were brilliant with something he alone seemed to know.

"You were particularly concerned," he said softly, "because they're *my* children."

She hesitated, snared by the impact of his gaze. It seemed to caress her, confine her, force from her truths she knew were safer kept to herself.

"And you were concerned about me." He leaned forward to nuzzle her cheek. "Why?"

He had placed a hand at her back and was rubbing gently. The motion was both soothing and provocative.

She arched slightly in response, the tips of her breasts coming in contact with the flannel of his shirt as she did so. A feeling like electric shock ran along her nerves. She sat still, afraid to move.

"I'd care about...anyone in...in danger." *Like myself,* she thought desperately. *Be sensible, Kellen. This isn't real. It cannot be. He lives in Connecticut with two boys who still love their mother. It can't...*

He leaned away from her for a moment to pull off his shirt, then his T-shirt. Then, his eyes never leaving hers, he wrapped both arms around her slowly and pulled her against him.

Rightness swept over her, filled her, soothed her as he enfolded her in his embrace and simply held her. A sighing little breath escaped her—along with every protest she'd clung to. She belonged in this man's arms.

"Oh, Dominic," she breathed against his collarbone. She didn't know what else to say, how to explain how right this felt.

"Kellen!" he whispered, his mouth against her ear. And she knew she didn't have to explain. Everything she felt was alive in his touch, resonant in his quiet cry of her name. Then he added, "I love you. I *love* you."

She felt as though her entire body became liquid at the sound of the words. Her heart melted, desire pooled bubbling hot at the heart of her, and her limbs lost all solidity.

Truth erupted from her. "I love you, too," she cried, wrapping her arms around his neck. "Oh, Dominic. I love you, too."

He unfastened the frail hooks of her bra, relishing the deeply desperate sound of her voice. She was as lost as he was in what they felt, and considerably more frightened. He didn't mind that. He would teach her not to be frightened of his love. But he liked that it made her hold him with such need, that it made her writhe in his arms when he stroked her, that what she felt for him made her pink and flushed from cheek to toe.

He liked that she was the one to pull back from him to toss the bra aside, that she closed the few inches between them with awed eagerness, and shuddered when he held her close.

Her nipples beaded against him and she uttered a little gasp into the hollow of his throat. For a moment, all he needed was to hold her, to know that they'd finally come to this, to feel her small hands splayed against his back and holding him as though afraid he might escape.

Now that she had finally acknowledged her love for Dominic, the intensity of the feeling seemed to have tripled inside her. It was as though a valve had opened, freeing emotion long suppressed. It leapt inside her like a geyser, moving fast and reaching high.

He pushed her gently back to the mattress, tugging her slacks and panties off, dragging the loose moccasins on her feet with them as he dropped them over the side of the bed.

He toed off his tennis shoes, then stripped off the rest of his clothes, dropping them beside hers.

He turned back to her, and saw a sight he suspected would warm him for the rest of his days. She lay watching him, a small, enigmatic smile on her face, and when her eyes met his, she opened her arms to him. He went into them, knowing without a doubt that he became hers at that moment. *Now,* he thought, running a hand down the length of her. *To make her mine.*

Kellen felt the banked energy in his fingertips, the passion held in check as he stroked every plane of her body. It thrummed from him into her and followed the path his hands took as they moved from her thigh to her hip to her breast and back again with tenderness and possession.

She felt his muscled back under her hands, the straight line of his waist and hip, his taut buttocks. The perfection of him made her feel a sense of wonder and a shameless greed.

"Mine," she said, her lips against his shoulder. "You're mine."

He found the words almost as sweet as her declaration of love, and the fierceness in her eyes when she spoke them almost as exciting as her wandering hands.

"Damn right," he said, reaching gently, artfully, inside her. She raised against his hand instantly, like a flower to the sun. "And you're mine. All mine."

"Yes," she promised. "Yes."

He rewarded her with his careful attention, his lips, his hands moving over and in her like a breath of wind, a stroke of suede, a kiss from the sun itself.

Kellen felt the world recede and her focus tighten on the smooth revolution of this little moment in time. The moment softened like a scene caught in slow motion, trying to capture all its magic, to enclose it in its arms, to bring it closer, closer, tighter until all that existed was that taunting, promising circle, spinning, spinning.

When she thought she couldn't bear it another moment, taunting turned to pleasure and the little circle flew apart, filling her being, lighting her world, revealing the universal truth. Love was everything.

Dominic held her against him as her body quaked, then entered her as the last little ripples eddied. She welcomed him, pulsed around him, drew him deeper.

He'd wanted to bring her to pleasure again, but it came upon him with swiftness and force. He tried to control it, to channel it back to her, but she fought him with delicious determination, pushing on him until he was forced to turn onto his back and settle her comfortably as she came with him.

But comfortable did not describe what he felt. Starving, desperate, needy, were more accurate.

She laced her fingers through his and began to move on him, leaning, swaying, turning until he felt engorged with passion, with need, with her.

For an instant, he enjoyed her startled expression when the promise of pleasure began to rise in her again. She gasped, clinging to him as her little contractions tightened around him. He swayed and circled with her, into the powerful spin that finally tightened into itself and exploded. Wracked with pleasure for long moments, he drifted back to earth just as she collapsed against him, breathing hard, whispering his name.

He pulled her down beside him, then reached over the edge of the bed for the blankets she had dropped there. He shook them out, leaned over to turn off the table lamp, then lay back beside Kellen, pulling her into his shoulder, tucking the blankets around them.

In the darkness, all the little domestic sounds of a functioning household drifted around them—the hum of the refrigerator, the tick of a clock, the sound of children turning over in bed.

He heard the same sounds at home every night, but there was no woman in his arms. It had been a revelation to him after Betsy died, that all the things they'd shared seemed to have changed in nature now that he was alone. The homey sounds had lost their cozy warmth; they simply kept him awake. When he heard the boys turn over in their beds, he had to get up to investigate, wondering if they were troubled or ill. Betsy had seemed always to be able to tell by the sound.

It had been necessary to go on without her; the boys needed him, and she had worked so hard for so long so that he would have the opportunity to do *his* work. He felt he had to continue it. But most of life had lost its lustre from his single point of view.

Now he had it back. Though much of his time with Kellen had been spent in a dark tunnel, she'd brought back the light into his life. He felt energy returning, dreams building again, a future beckoning.

But she would fight him on it, he knew, so he wouldn't bring it up again until it was time.

"I love you," he said softly, squeezing her close and kissing her temple.

She tightened her grip on his neck and kissed his throat. "I love you."

Kellen spoke the words with complete conviction, dispelling from her thoughts any consequences connected with them. She couldn't, wouldn't think beyond this moment. It was too beautiful, too renewing, too filled with the glow that seldom lighted her quiet little life.

She still felt as though she'd walked into a storybook two nights ago, and begun to live her life with the characters who populated it.

Only now, her nerve endings still rippling with the sensations Dominic had made her feel, her body still tender from accepting his, she had no doubt whatsoever that the *prince* was real.

THE FIRST SHOUT woke him. "Dad! Daaaad!"

Dominic heard it in his subconscious and came awake already reaching for the gun he'd tucked right under his side of the bed. He had a vague impression of an instant of entanglement before he was on his feet, gun in hand, racing for the bedroom.

He saw the light go on just before he reached the room, then collided with Travis as the boy raced into the hallway, apparently on his way to roust him.

"Ethan's got him, Dad!" Travis shouted excitedly, turning to follow him into the room. "Ethan's got Mueller!"

Dominic stopped in the middle of the room, gun braced in the palm of his free hand, taking a precious moment to see precisely what was happening before he perforated Mueller for trying to get his kids.

He blinked at what he saw, then focused again, certain he was mistaken. But he wasn't.

Ethan stood on the bed in the T-shirt with the rose on it, holding a leg that protruded from the high window above. Ethan had a foot braced against the wall and was pulling on the leg with all his might.

The leg was clad in denim and on the foot, kicking wildly in Ethan's grasp, was a black walking shoe.

Beyond the window, he could hear shouts, threats, and profanity.

Dominic covered the small distance between them in three long strides, noticing what Ethan was too busy to see; the foot was much too small to be a man's.

Dominic put the gun back into his belt and pushed Ethan gently aside. "All right, I've got her, Son."

Dominic slid the window up and was immediately struck in the face by something hard and solid. A square leather purse fell to the bed. Then a hand came through the opening and reached for his face, curled to scratch. Meanwhile, the foot continued to flail.

He got a firm grip on the foot and the hand and pulled.

A slight gray-haired woman fell into his waiting arms with a scream. As she kicked and flailed, Dominic smiled. A glimpse of her face and an armful of her attitude told him precisely who she was.

"Mrs. Clark?" he asked.

The action stopped and for a moment they were frozen in a ridiculous tableau—Travis standing beside the bed, Ethan on it beside Dominic, who held a middle-aged woman in midkick in his arms.

"Who the hell are you?" the woman demanded. "And where is my daughter?"

"Mom!" Kellen cried from somewhere behind him. "Mom, what are you doing here? Oh, Dominic! Get her down here."

Kellen continued to give orders as she helped Dominic down, the burden of her mother still in his arms. He carried her through to the living room and placed her on the rumpled sofa bed.

"Mom! Mom!" Kellen sat beside her, taking her hand. "Are you all right? Say something."

"Am I all right?" the woman finally replied, voice raised. "Are *you* all right, is the question. I've been trying to phone you for days." Mary Ellen's voice quieted and she swallowed, her voice heavy with maternal concern. "I was beginning to think you'd been kidnapped and murdered."

Kellen wrapped her arms around her and laughed softly. "Kidnapped, yes. Murdered, no. At least not yet."

"What?" Mary Ellen held her away and looked into her eyes, obviously confused. "Who kidnapped you?"

Kellen pointed to Dominic. "He did."

"You *did?*" Ethan and Travis asked in unison.

Dominic gave Kellen a scolding look.

"And you are?" Mary Ellen asked imperiously, then, as he opened his mouth to reply, peered more closely at him and answered her own question with a look of incredulity. "Dominic Hunter . . . the writer."

Annoyed that her mother had recognized him when she hadn't, that reality had invaded this perfect night, that she now had to answer for things and find answers *to* things that were all difficult, Kellen diverted her mother's attention from Dominic.

"Why were you breaking into my house?"

Mary Ellen turned to her with a frown. "Because you hadn't answered my calls, Joanie was out of town, so I came to see for myself what was going on. I could see that your van wasn't here, that everything was dark—so I was doing like they do in the detective shows. I was going to try to find your calendar to see who your last appointment was before you disappeared."

Kellen rolled her eyes. "Mom, that's so theatrical."

"She was desperate," Dominic said gently, coming to stand over Kellen's mother with an apologetic smile. "I'm sorry about your leg. My son thought you were an intruder."

Ethan, at the foot of the sofa bed with Travis, shrugged and winced. "I'm really sorry. I thought for sure you were Mueller."

"I heard you say that before," Mary Ellen said with a wry smile in the boy's direction, "while you were dislocating my knee, I think." She turned to Dominic. "Who is Mueller?"

"The man who's after Dominic," Kellen replied offhandedly.

"After Dominic? Why?" Mary Ellen asked, then her eyes widened as an answer occurred to her. "Does it have something to do with the Morley case you're working on now?''

Surprised that she knew the nature of his current project, he nodded. ''The court convicted the wrong man.''

''You mean, Morley didn't do it?''

''No.''

Mary Ellen sat up, taking hold of his wrist and pulling him down in front of Kellen. ''I just read all about you in *People*. But they said you were in Belize, studying ancient Mayan ruins.''

He nodded. ''My agent put out that story when he hired someone to hide me.''

She frowned as though something didn't compute. ''He's hiding you in my daughter's house?''

''I'll put on a pot of coffee,'' Kellen said, wanting no part in the explanation that must follow. She beckoned to the boys. ''Come on, guys. I'll make you some hot chocolate.''

Ethan and Travis followed Kellen as she ground coffee beans, placed them into the coffee filter, prepared the pot then plugged it in.

''Dad kidnapped you?'' Ethan asked.

''Not exactly.'' She explained about Spike and Gordy. ''Your father said he'd be able to handle being locked in the house better if he had me...'' She paused to think about putting the reason diplomatically. ''If he had me...for company,'' she said, pleased with her easy prevarication.

''So they took him literally.''

Travis, standing as close to her elbow as he could get, watched her every move. ''What's literally?''

"They thought he really meant it," Ethan explained.

"Didn't he?" Travis asked.

"He meant he'd really like company," Kellen went on, moving to get the kettle from the stove to fill it. The boys followed her as though they were all attached. "But he didn't mean he wanted them to kidnap me to...to keep him company."

"Were you scared?" Travis asked.

"At first," she admitted, pulling the full kettle out from under the tap and replacing the lid. She turned to the stove and they followed her again. "But your father was very upset with them and nice to me, so I wasn't afraid anymore."

"Why didn't he send you home?"

"Because by then he thought Mueller was out there somewhere and if he let me go, Mueller would get me and try to make me tell him where your father was."

"He was trying to protect her," Ethan told his brother.

"What did you guys do?" Travis wanted to know.

"Your father worked on his book," she said, getting cups down, finding it difficult to discuss those first few hours when the fairy tale began to unfold. She wondered if that was because she knew it would have to end soon. "And I sat on the sofa in his office. Then your father made me breakfast."

Travis looked horrified. "Didn't he let you sleep?"

She had a sudden, sharply vivid memory of all the times she'd slept in his arms over the past few days and nights and felt desolate at the realization that that wouldn't go on forever.

"I slept on the sofa while he worked."

Ever practical, Travis asked, "Didn't *he* sleep?"

"I think you're asking too many questions," Ethan said. When Kellen turned to look at him, he smiled at her significantly. She smiled back innocently, refusing to give credence to his apparent suspicions. "No, it's all right. Your father had a lot on his mind, Travis. He was worried about the two of you, and about me. He didn't sleep very much while he was at the house."

"Are you coming home with us?" Travis asked outright.

She looked down into his questioning little face, all blond and freckled and curious and replied easily, "No, I'm not. I live here in Sandpiper."

She pulled a package of blueberry muffins down from the top of the refrigerator.

The boys were silent. She wished she understood what was going on in their minds.

"We have horses," Travis finally said, his tone suggesting he was offering an enticement.

"And flowers," Ethan added, a little eagerly, she thought. "In the spring, there's dogwood and mountain laurel."

"Your father told me a little bit about it." She tried not to remember her cruel comments about where he lived. "It sounds beautiful."

"And our house is a lot, lot bigger than this," Travis boasted.

"Trav," Ethan said with disgust, "that's a stupid thing to say. This is a nice little house. Kellen is letting us stay here. You shouldn't say bad things about it."

"I didn't mean it was bad." Travis was quick to defend himself. "I just meant if she came to live with us, she'd have lots more room." He pointed to the stack of boxes in the corner. "She'd have a place to put all that stuff."

Kellen put a soothing hand on Ethan's arm and ruffled Travis's hair. "I know what you meant, Travis. You didn't hurt my feelings. That's all the stuff I work with and it would be nice to have a place to put it."

"We even have three bedrooms that are for guests because we don't have enough people to fill them up," Travis boasted.

"Dad says you're coming to have Thanksgiving with us."

Kellen halved and buttered muffins, giving the task her full attention. She didn't let the image of herself at the Hunter Thanksgiving table form in her mind. She found herself wanting to see the horses and the flowers.

"He's mistaken, Ethan," she said mildly. "I have work to do here. I can't just leave."

"You could just come for a weekend," Travis coaxed, standing so close to her she could barely wield the butter knife. "Dad has a friend that could fly you back home. He flies Dad around all the time."

"It's really pretty now," Ethan added. "Some of the leaves have fallen, but a lot of them haven't and their colors are really beautiful."

"And Mrs. Gibbons would cook and clean for you like she does for us," Travis chattered.

Kellen handed him half a muffin, hoping to quiet him. He just talked around it. "You wouldn't have to do anything except have fun. We could take you Rollerblading."

Ethan rolled his eyes. "She wouldn't want to go Rollerblading. She'd want to go to the theater, and to fancy places for dinner, and to take long walks along the river. Like Mom used to do."

Travis looked up in surprise. "Do you like to do that stuff, too?"

She couldn't lie into that open little face. "Yes. I do."

He accepted that, though it was obvious he couldn't understand it. "Ladies are weird."

The kettle sang and she dispatched Ethan to turn it off, while asking Travis to carry the plate of muffins into the living room. She went to spoon cocoa mixture into cups, then asked Ethan to pour water into them while she poured coffee.

"Dad says you're coming," Ethan declared. "And things usually turn out the way he thinks they should."

Unwilling to diminish his faith in his father, Kellen declined to argue. Putting all the cups on a tray, she carried them into the living room, Ethan following with a clutch of napkins.

Dominic or her mother had folded the sofa bed, Kellen noted as she passed around cups. Dominic sat in the room's only big chair, Carrot asleep in his lap, and her mother was curled into a corner of the sofa, leaning on the pile of blankets and pillows placed there. They were chatting and laughing cozily. She wasn't sure she liked that.

Mary Ellen smiled knowingly into Kellen's face as she took a cup from the tray. Then she reached up with her free hand to pinch Kellen's cheek.

"Well, sweetie. I'm glad to know that you finally have a grasp on what life is really all about."

Kellen looked up at Dominic, her cheeks growing pink. He had *told* her?

He returned her look with one of bland innocence.

"I understand you've been quite a trooper," Mary Ellen said, then blew daintily into her cup to dispel any suggestion of double entendre. "Despite the danger, you stayed right by Dominic's side every moment."

Ethan swallowed a large bite of muffin and praised enthusiastically, "She jumped on me when I mistook Dad for one of Mueller's men and jumped on *him*. I had a hard time fighting her off until Travis jumped on top of *her*."

Mary Ellen shook her head, a small smile curving before she took a sip of coffee. "My, my. Sounds like quite a fracas. Where did this happen?"

"At the house where Dad had been hiding."

Mary Ellen nodded as she contemplated her muffin half. "That lodgelike place on the hill where the police said they found Kellen's van."

"Right."

Kellen saw Dominic stop with his cup halfway to his lips, his expression changing from one of interest to the granite-jaw look she remembered from their time in the tunnel.

He reached over to put his cup down. Carrot meowed at the disturbance and leapt off his lap.

"How do you know what the place looks like?" he asked.

"Well, I was just there," Mary Ellen replied conversationally. "When I got to Sandpiper I went to the police because I didn't know what to think. I described her van and they told me they'd found it at that house. They'd gone in response to a call about gunfire. So, I went to look for myself."

Dominic was on his feet in an instant, grabbing each boy by an arm and pushing them toward the kitchen, encouraging Kellen and Mary Ellen to follow.

"Dad, what...?"

"Dominic, what's the matter?" Kellen resisted.

"She went to the house," he said sharply, continuing to herd all of them as he spoke. "Then she came immediately here. If anyone from the house saw her and followed her here..."

"But I didn't see anyone," Mary Ellen insisted.

"Out to the truck?" Ethan asked as they approached the back door.

Before Dominic could reply, the door to the back exploded inward, admitting four men in impeccable suits, and carrying semiautomatic weapons.

One came forward to look condescendingly around the modest kitchen, then rested his eyes on Dominic with a cold smile.

"Well, Hunter," Mueller said in a quiet, even voice. "One would think you've been avoiding me."

Chapter Ten

"I was becoming concerned," Mueller said smoothly as he advanced on Dominic, who stood his ground, Travis clutching his arm, Ethan on his other side, "that we were never going to get together. And we have so much to talk about."

"I have nothing to tell you that you don't already know," Dominic said. "It's the police I'm anxious to talk to."

Mueller shook his head with all apparent regret. "I'm afraid you won't be doing that. Nobody will...." He put a hand to Travis's head as he spoke. Dominic hit him squarely in the jaw, his fist connecting with an ugly thud.

Mueller reeled backward into the arms of the men behind him.

"Don't touch anyone who belongs to me," Dominic warned, "or I'll kill you."

Another man immediately stepped forward, prepared to swing his big gun at Dominic's face. Dominic grabbed Ethan's arm, preventing his interception, at the same moment that Mueller shouted for them to stop.

"I need him coherent, Carter," he said sharply. "I want to know just what he's done about what he knows."

"I have a taped conversation with Carolyn Bowles," he lied, "in a safety deposit box."

Mueller yanked the gun from Carter and waggled the barrel under Dominic's chin. "Then there must be a key."

Dominic nodded. "Must be."

Mueller placed the tip of the weapon against Ethan's chest. "Where is it?"

Kellen's mouth was dry, her heart thumping with fear, but Ethan said defiantly, "Don't tell 'em, Dad. I'm not afraid of him."

"I mailed it to my agent." Dominic replied calmly, though a pulse ticked at his temple.

Mueller looked doubtful, then angry. "You wouldn't do that. Mail's too uncertain."

"That's right. You'd never find it until it arrived. And by then you'll be in a jail cell."

Mueller's men grinned at one another. Mueller indicated with an inclination of his head, the gun held against Ethan's chest. "There's something you don't know about me and the police."

Dominic nodded. "But I do. I found the commissioner's foreign bank account and all the checks from you he's deposited in it. I'm sure it was much easier for you to operate with him on your side. But things are about to turn on you."

Mueller blanched but looked him in the eye. "Things don't turn on me. Sometimes they cause me a few anxious moments, but they always turn out my way."

Ethan snickered. "This time they won't. My dad always gets things *his* way."

"Good Lord!" Mary Ellen exclaimed loudly, stepping forward. Mueller moved the gun from Ethan's chest to hers. Kellen felt her already rocketing heart leap into her throat. "You sound like a bully on a playground." She gave the barrel of the gun a slap out of her way. "And don't point that at me. I intend to die an old lady on a cruise ship somewhere between two romantic ports of call. I'm not going to be blown to bits by some two-bit hood in a designer suit." She ran a disparaging gaze down his natty attire. "That looks just too polished. Perfection doesn't appeal to anyone. Particularly not to women."

"Lady." Mueller shoved her back with the barrel of the gun. "Shut up. I wouldn't go to someone in denim for fashion consultation, thank you very much. Who are you, anyway?"

Mary Ellen pointed to Kellen. "I'm her mother."

Mueller raised an eyebrow. "The hooker's mother?"

Kellen sighed, caught between terror and extreme annoyance. Ignoring her mother's startled look, she opened her mouth to deny that she was or ever had been a hooker—then had a second thought. One she might regret, she realized, but one that suddenly seemed better than waiting for Mueller to cut loose with his weapon.

She stepped forward, as close to Mueller as his weapon would allow her, and tucked her index finger under the knot on his silk tie.

"I think it's a very seductive look," she cooed, sweeping her lashes down then up as she pretended to relish a slow examination of his pristine appearance. "Don't listen to Mother. She doesn't know anything about it. I for one find the look very..." She leaned a little closer, her eyes languid, and said softly, "... provocative."

"Kellen..." Dominic warned softly.

Kellen ignored him.

Mueller appeared unmoved. "You expect me to buy that?"

She smiled into his eyes, the coldness she saw there causing her a little difficulty in holding the smile. "Of course not. For you, I'll give it away. What do you say? A little..." She let a smile supply the word. "For my freedom?"

"A little what?" Travis asked loudly. "Dad, what's she talking about?"

Dominic was aware of Mary Ellen looking nervously at him. He knew what Kellen was doing. Divide and conquer. If she got Mueller out of the room, she obviously trusted herself to handle him while he, Dominic, somehow took care of the other three.

Still, he couldn't let her proceed with what he guessed was her plan. But he had another idea.

"What do you say?" Kellen was asking Mueller. "He's not going to challenge your men with his children in the room, and I'll tell you..." she hesitated suggestively "...and show you...everything I know."

Dominic snickered, putting his hands in his pockets. "Get it in writing that she isn't going to charge you," he said to Mueller. "Not only is she higher than market value, but...well..." he shrugged, as though suddenly overtaken by gentlemanly reticence "...she's...kind of an amateur."

Kellen rounded on him as he'd hoped she would.

She glared at him, her eyes telling him that she was trying to accomplish something here and how dare he interfere. They also told him he was going to pay for that slur.

"Amateur?" she asked coolly.

"Amateur," he replied, also trying to send her a message with his eyes. *I'm not going to let you leave the room with Mueller, so shut up and follow my lead.* "I mean, it was all right, if you don't mind having to provide directions."

He was vaguely aware of the startled looks on his children. He was comforted by the knowledge that Travis had no idea what they were talking about, and Ethan had probably figured out he had a plan at work here.

Mary Ellen looked completely confused.

Kellen got the message. Her plan would have worked better, she was sure, but Dominic's seemed to be louder and was less revolting to consider, so she played along.

She faced him, hands on her hips. "I don't remember you complaining. In fact, when we were in the tunnel, I seem to recall your willingness to trade the last spoonful of paté for it."

"I'm a meat and potatoes man," he said. "I'd have traded paté for a good steak."

"Folks..." Mueller broke in, trying to reach between them to wedge them apart.

But Kellen grabbed Dominic by his shirtfront and waggled a small fist at him. "Yeah, well, maybe you'd like a little of this up your potato nose."

"Thanks, I'm not into violence." Dominic pretended to prod her on, his eyes telling her to go with it, to do what he seemed to be encouraging. "Mueller, however, might be just your style." He turned to his adversary with a man-to-man grin. "She likes a little rough handling, a good swat now and then."

Still clutching his shirtfront, Kellen read his eyes and found herself suddenly, paralyzingly afraid. Not of doing what he wanted her to do, but of what would result afterward. Could they pull it off?

"You take that back!" she demanded, buying time.

He shook his head. "Too late for that," he said significantly. "We both know how it is, Kellen."

She slapped him hard with her open hand. Mueller came between them to pull them apart. Dominic came up with both hands locked and slammed them under his chin. He reeled backward again, his gun firing at the ceiling, raining plaster down on them like snow.

Ethan and Travis leapt in unison on one man, while Mary Ellen swung at Carter with a pot she grabbed off the stove. Kellen leapt at a fourth man, reaching for the knife with which she'd sliced the muffins.

They landed hard on the cold linoleum. She felt her hair pulled as the man tried to yank her off him. The knife flew out of her hands as she struggled. It occurred to her in a corner of her mind detached from the struggle that hand-to-hand combat wasn't as easy as it appeared to be on television.

Then there was another spate of gunfire and the man, wide-eyed, stopped struggling. A stockinged foot prodded him off of Kellen and Dominic reached down to pull her to her feet. In his free hand was one of the weapons. The floor was littered with Mueller and his men, and Ethan stood over them with one of the guns, Travis at his side, and Mary Ellen with another.

The back door burst open again, and Dominic turned to it, raising the weapon while he shoved Kellen behind him.

A parade of burly men in overcoats and hats walked into the kitchen. Kellen gasped, but Dominic laughed softly and lowered his weapon, stepping forward to walk into the first man's open arms.

"Well!" the man announced in a deep baritone. "You always were an overachiever. I don't know why I bothered to come to your rescue."

"Well, I'm glad you're here Uncle Rocco!"

THE MEN IN the overcoats removed the men in the suits who turned them over to men in uniforms who arrived shortly after.

The kitchen was flooded with sunlight by the time Mueller and his men had been dispensed with. It was noon by the time they'd given the police their reports.

The boys were asleep on their feet, and Kellen found herself leaning heavily on Dominic.

"I think you're going to need a place with more beds to spend tonight," Rocco said with the blustery good humor Kellen was learning defined him. "I'll make stuffed manicotti for dinner." He turned to Dominic as though they hadn't just apprehended a dangerous murderer and saved five people from imminent death. "Is there sauce in the freezer?"

Dominic laughed wearily, holding Kellen to him. "Yes. the Italian bread'll be three days old by now, though."

"Small detail. I'll take you to the house, then go back to the market for fresh parmesan, olive oil, and salad greens."

Rocco drove Dominic, the boys, Kellen, Mary Ellen and Carrot back to the house where Dominic had been held, and where Kellen had spent the first night of her storybook adventure. Mary Ellen shooed Dominic and Kellen away, and promised to see the boys and the cat to bed and find a place to curl up herself.

Rocco nodded gallantly. "Permit me to see to your comfort."

That sounded a little ambiguous to Kellen, but her mother didn't seem to mind. She simply smiled demurely and followed with an arm around Ethan as Rocco lifted Travis off his feet and carried him upstairs.

It was going to be over, Kellen though as Dominic led her into the bedroom and closed the door. In a matter of hours it would all be over. The romance, the adventure, the warmth . . . the love.

They climbed under the covers in their underwear, and curled up together in peaceful silence.

Kellen thought she should say something, tell him how knowing him had changed her life forever, but that would be admitting that it would be over when she awoke. And she didn't want it to be.

So she simply curled up in his arms, committed the warmth and security of the experience to memory so that she could pull it out later when she climbed again into her lonely bed. She nuzzled into his neck for what she expected would be the last time, and drifted off.

Dominic felt the tension in her despite her weariness, and he thought he knew what was at the bottom of it. She was going to fight him on going to Connecticut. It occurred to him to set her straight now, this minute. To tell her he wasn't leaving without her. But he was too tired to argue—and he was sure she would argue. It could wait until later, when they awoke.

A dark blue dusk filled the room when Kellen opened her eyes. A wonderful aroma filled with Italian spices wafted up the stairs and, she was sure, through every crevice and into every nostril in the house. Rocco's manicotti was in the oven. And probably garlic bread.

She raised her head off Dominic's shoulder and found that even in the darkness, she could see the spark of wit and warmth in his dark eyes. She had a sudden, vivid flash of the hours they'd spent in the tunnel, and longed for what the fates never allowed— the opportunity to relive it.

She would be less rigid this time, more open, more accepting of the fact that falling in love with Dominic would change her.

"Good morning," he said softly, reaching a gentle hand up to push the veil of dark hair back from one side of her face. She felt that little touch to her very core and committed it, too, to her collection of memories.

"It's nighttime," she corrected with a little laugh.

"No," he said gravely. "It's been night for a long, long time. But when I woke up with you in my arms, the sun came up. You've brought morning to my life, Kellen."

"Dominic . . ." she began to protest on a whisper.

But he pulled her down to him and kissed her long and tenderly. He didn't want to hear her arguments now. He wanted to remind her how much he loved her, how good they were together. He wanted to weaken her defenses.

He rolled over with her until she lay under him, then he ran his hands over every quivering inch of her, felt her come to life under his touch.

Kellen wanted so much to make love with him this last time. She already remembered every little move he made, the reverent yet possessive way he touched her, the feel of his lips on hers, on her throat, on her breasts, on her belly. But this time would have to live with her forever.

She wanted it to go slowly so that she could savor every intimate moment, every tiny personal detail; but her passion for Dominic was already like a river at flood tide, running too wild and too fast to contain, spilling over all boundaries, rushing toward its destiny to cover every living thing.

Dominic felt the love in her body, and saw it in her eyes. But there was a sadness in her touch, a quiet longing in her eyes. She reached for him, drew him toward her, stroked and caressed him with the knowledge of a woman who'd lain beside him for years rather than just one time.

He understood that, because the moment he'd touched her, he'd felt as though he'd known her always, as though they'd met in another life—or as though Betsy had sent her to him.

"We're going to grow old together, Kellen," he said, his voice heavy with desire as he entered her in one swift thrust. "I promise you."

Kellen wrapped every part of herself around him and held him with every ounce of strength she possessed. She closed her ears to the promise, knowing the storybook was about to close. But unwilling to relinquish one particle of the fantasy until the very last page.

UNCLE ROCCO SERVING manicotti with a white tablecloth wrapped around his waist was a sight to behold. Kellen found it hard to think of him as some kind of crime boss.

She watched him ladle extra sauce on the boys' plates, croon over them like a sweet old grandmother, then wrap an arm around Dominic's shoulders and laugh heartily, obviously relieved and grateful that his favorite nephew was safe, after all.

His manicotti was the best she'd ever tasted, and she'd had it in a little restaurant in Florence with her mother the summer she'd graduated from college. It was entirely possible, she thought fancifully, that he controlled his corner of the south side of Chicago with his culinary skills. Shopkeepers paid protection or they got none of the sauce he'd learned to make at his mother's elbow.

"You mean they're *all* fine?" Dominic was asking. "Mueller didn't..."

Rocco shook his head as he took his place at the table beside Mary Ellen. "Mueller had Gordy and the men I sent out to check on you locked in the basement of an empty summer cottage they'd taken over. Gordy had a black eye and a few broken ribs from the original struggle when they took him. Hospital says he's fine. He's flying home with us tomorrow."

"And Spike and Burton?" Kellen asked.

"Also fine. Mueller never had them. Spike got picked up by the police for speeding the day he took Burton to the hospital. They held him first because of Burton's gunshot wound, then they discovered he had a record and they became suspicious. Unfortunately, Burton was sedated and couldn't corroborate his story that you were in trouble. It all sounded fantastic to them. By the time some conscientious cop checked with your agent like Spike kept pleading for him to do, he learned the truth. By then, I was already here."

"What about Burton's men? We couldn't raise them on the radio."

"Would you believe a dead battery in the radio?" Rocco looked amused. "I told you not to trust the Manhattan Security Company. I have a feeling heads will roll."

"I've been wondering how Mrs. Bowles managed to escape Mueller," Dominic said. "He had to be watching her if he saw me stop there."

Rocco nodded. "She told me that after she talked to you she became paranoid that someone might have seen you together and that she'd put herself in danger. She never went home that night. She 'borrowed' jeans and a sweater and a shopping bag from her hostess. She left the party with them hidden in the mink coat over her arm. She changed in an elevator and took a bus out of town and went to a spa for a week. Whoever Mueller had watching her probably mistook her for a domestic when she left the building that night. My boys found her because the bus driver remembered seeing a mink coat in her shopping bag and wondered if she'd stolen it."

"But, didn't Burton's company or Dad's agent get worried when nobody with Dad reported in? Why didn't they call the police or the sheriff or something?" Ethan asked between bites of manicotti.

"We still didn't want the police involved at that point because the commissioner was one of Mueller's partners. So they called me. I was already on the way because of you two. And speaking of which..." Rocco folded large arms on the table and glowered at his great-nephews.

Ethan and Travis looked at each other in concern, then to their father for support.

"They were disobedient and reckless," Dominic judged sternly.

Kellen gasped indignantly beside him. "They came to your rescue!"

Dominic gave her a glance that told her he was pleased with her support of his boys, but he didn't need it to evaluate their behavior. "But they showed courage and resourcefulness," he praised, letting his eyes light on each one for a moment, letting himself drink in the perfection of their sturdy beings and the fact that all the unthinkable things that might have happened hadn't. "And I'd missed them so much. I was damn glad to see them."

The boys relaxed visibly.

"What I don't understand," Travis piped up, "was all that stuff when Mueller was here about a hooker. What is that?"

Everyone stared at their plates, except Kellen who watched Dominic with interest.

Dominic took the question in stride; it was hardly the worst one Travis had ever asked.

"It's a woman who makes love with a man for money," he replied matter-of-factly.

Travis nodded knowledgeably. "That's hugging and kissing in bed and stuff."

"Right." Dominic nodded, praying he didn't ask him to define "and stuff."

"So, is that bad?" Travis asked. He looked at Ethan who was groaning, then at Mary Ellen as she put a hand over her eyes and concentrated on her salad. "I mean, to love somebody?"

"It kind of depends on how you look at it," Dominic replied, hoping this was Travis's last question. "Usually, that's the kind of thing married people do, or people who love each other very, very much. That's how they show their love. But some people don't have anybody, and so they pay someone to love them."

"But you and Kellen do love each other, don'tcha?" He smiled as he asked the question. Then he frowned again. "So why did he think Kellen was somebody who does that?"

"We talked about that last night," Kellen said. "Remember? When we were making cocoa? I told you Spike and Gordy had misunderstood your father and kidnapped me to bring me to him. I guess Mueller knew your dad had come out without a lady, so when he saw me with him, that's what he thought."

"Oh." Travis considered that a moment then went back to his manicotti, apparently satisfied.

Dominic sighed, then grinned at Kellen. "Thank you," he said.

She smiled. "You're welcome."

"So." Rocco stood and began clearing away plates. Everyone rose to help him. "We'll have a quick dessert, then I want everyone to go back to bed and get a good night's sleep. You ladies need your beauty sleep. Our flight leaves at eleven a.m. and it's a good hour and a half to the airport, so we'll have to be up early."

The news hit Kellen like a sledge. She'd known it was coming, of course, it was just that it wasn't really fact until the words were spoken.

Kellen opened her mouth to announce calmly that she wasn't going when Rocco's words registered.

"What do you mean 'ladies?'" She'd just placed her plate and cup on the counter and turned to Dominic, her frown defensive and argumentative.

Before he could reply, Mary Ellen said, her eyes sparkling with excitement, "Dominic invited me while you were helping Rocco with the salad. I've always wanted to get back to New England for a book I want to do about colonial inns."

Her mother being invited to Connecticut, too, was an element in this Kellen hadn't considered when she'd planned her arguments. Confused for a moment, she could do nothing but state the obvious.

"What about clothes? What about—"

"Not a problem," Dominic said, walking past her with a platter he handed to Ethan, who was rinsing dishes and handing them to Rocco who stacked the dishwasher.

Kellen grabbed his arm as he turned to go back to the table. "How can clothes not be a problem?" she asked, an edge of sarcasm in her tone because of her extreme annoyance. He'd invited her mother deliberately, she was sure, so that she, Kellen, wouldn't fight him on going herself. How could she refuse if her mother was going? Well, he was about to see. "Do you live in a nudist colony?"

Travis, collecting silverware in a dishpan, turned to giggle at the silly suggestion. Dominic quelled him with a look.

"I'll take care of what you need when we get there," he told her.

"I have a bag in my rental car at Kellen's," Mary Ellen said.

"It's a crime scene." Dominic didn't want Kellen going anywhere near her house again for fear he'd lose her. "They won't let you take anything from the house, or from anything parked on the property."

Kellen looked at him suspiciously. "That's only for dead bodies, isn't it?"

Before he could confirm or deny that, she asked, "And if we were involved in a crime, how come we can leave at all?"

"We've given our reports, Mueller will be extradited to Boston," Dominic replied mildly. "Eventually, we'll both have to testify. For now, we're free to go."

"Fine." She marched past him to the table and picked up the little bowl of freshly grated parmesan. "Then I'll go to Boston when it's time to testify. Right now I don't have time to go haring off to Connecticut."

"Why not?" Mary Ellen asked. She took the bowl from her and put it in the refrigerator.

"Because I have a business," she said, spreading both arms out in exasperation. "Because I have a life that does not involve Dominic Hunter!"

Even Rocco and the boys turned to look at her. The words had been so vehement, angry out of all proportion to her mother's simple question.

Mary Ellen faced her squarely.

"The time between Thanksgiving and Christmas is your slow period," she said, apparently having no compunction in correcting her in front of a room filled with people. "How many times have you told me that? Thanksgiving is three days away. I'm sure you have all your windows in by now."

"There's more to my life than my business," Kellen stated quietly, stiffly.

"No, there isn't," Mary Ellen argued.

Dominic took Kellen's arm and cast an apologetic look around the room. "Excuse us, please," he said and propelled her out of the kitchen and toward the stairs.

She went along cooperatively, refusing to give him the satisfaction of a struggle.

"I'm not going to Connecticut with you," she declared as he towed her up the stairs to the room they'd shared.

He waited until he'd closed the door behind them before refuting her statement.

"Yes, you are." He pushed her into the room's only chair near the bed and went to the French windows, opening them wide to let in the night air. It was cold and smelled like rain and the ocean. He drew a deep breath, suspecting he was going to need fortification. "Don't play this game with me."

"Game?" she repeated, quietly at first, then more loudly as the suggestion that she was somehow maneuvering him incensed her, "Game!" She went to the windows and grabbing his arm, yanked him around. "How dare you accuse me of such a thing? What do you call inviting my mother to Connecticut?"

He replied calmly, "An opportunity to get better acquainted with the woman who's going to be my mother-in-law."

"She is not going to be your mother-in-law," she snapped, hating his calm, wanting desperately for him to be as upset as she was. "But she may be your pallbearer if you don't stop this!"

He looked down at her as the chill evening air ruffled his hair and wound hers across her face and throat. He reached out to smooth it back.

"I will not stop," he said evenly. "Accept it, adjust to it, build your plans around it, because you're coming to Connecticut, and you're going to marry me."

He turned to push the doors closed, loathe to confine himself inside once more after so many days of being trapped but hating also to have their argument telegraphed to the neighborhood.

Afraid she would burst with sheer exasperation, Kellen tried another tack.

"Don't you see what's happened to you?" she asked reasonably, lowering her voice.

"Sure," he replied. "I've fallen in love."

"No, you haven't," she said authoritatively. "You're a victim of the classic bodyguard-lady-in-distress syndrome. We were confined together, forced to share wit and courage and sleeping bags, and presto—romance! Two people who ordinarily wouldn't give each other a second look are sharing life on very intimate terms. It's confusing. It feels like love, but actually it was just . . . necessity."

She had walked around him as she spoke, partly as a ploy to avoid his eyes, and partly because it helped her think logically. Every time he looked into her eyes, she felt as though he'd gotten a lock on her, as though some invisible beam in him closed over her and pulled her toward him and with him. And she didn't want to go to Connecticut.

He finally stopped her pacing by taking hold of her arm and pulling her firmly to the edge of the bed where he sat her down. His eyes were stormy and dark and deadly serious.

"You're telling me you didn't feel anything?" he asked, sitting beside her.

"Of course I did." She stared at her hands. "I had my own syndrome going. The quiet-unexciting-woman-walks-into-a-fairy-tale syndrome." She tried to make her voice sound dispassionate, removed. She added a sigh she felt had just the right degree of acceptance. "But now that it's over, I can see very clearly what happened. We were both living dreams, that's all. You were lonely, my life was just the same old—"

"Bull!" he said, rising off the bed as though he'd been ejected. He took several paces away from her, then several paces back, his control decimated. "We have had this 'it's real, it's not real' argument over and over. What is wrong with you? You think because a relationship is wonderful, it can't be real? Because two people happen to come from very different backgrounds and situations that what they feel has to be ignored? That's ridiculous!" He pointed to the bed. "You're saying that the love we made there this afternoon was some kind of phantom experience?" He leaned over her in emphasis and lowered his voice. "Kellen, you shook in my arms like a rose in a storm."

Kellen shot to her feet because he was right and that was what made it so hard.

"It feels real now!" she cried, tears beginning to clog her throat and burn her eyes. She ignored them, intent on making her point. "But to be real, it has to *last,* and I know that it can't."

He saw the emotion in her eyes, heard it in her voice, and made a valiant effort to calm his own frustration because she seemed completely sincere and he didn't understand why she should be.

"Why not?" he asked.

"Because my mother did the very thing we're arguing about," she said, memories of the father she'd adored and virtually lost to the divorce all those years ago rising up again. She'd been seven, adoring and sensitive and very, very lost when he explained he was leaving. "My parents are divorced," she said grimly.

"Kellen," he said, striving for reason, "I'm sorry. I'm sure that was hard for you. But half the population's parents are divorced."

Tears began to fall and she turned away from him, going to the French doors and opening them again. She wanted desperately to leap out to the mountain ash tree and escape, but she remembered what happened the last time she tried that.

She felt Dominic walk up behind her. The similarities between her relationship with Dominic and her parents' relationship were too remarkable to ignore.

"You don't understand. My mother met my father at a dude ranch she was listing in one of her first travel books," Kellen began, recounting the tale as she'd heard it so many times. "She wandered farther off than she should have on a horse she wasn't supposed to ride, and got lost. My father was the owner's son and a good tracker, so he was sent after her. By the time he found her, it was dark and they stayed in an old line cabin." She sighed, remembering how romantic she'd always thought the circumstances to be. "Mom always said it was like something out of a novel."

"Kellen, forgive me," Dominic interrupted, "but that's a hackneyed argument. Because their marriage failed doesn't mean ours would."

"Why not?" She braced her hands on the railing and though she was cold, she breathed deeply of the air, needing to clear her beleaguered brain. "They thought what they felt was real. So do we. What you don't know is that everyday life will invade and I'll turn out to be far less interesting than you thought I was, and you'll be just another guy who—" She stopped, knowing that part wasn't true. He'd always hold her heart.

He came around to stand beside her. She looked up into his eyes and dissolved into tears.

Dominic pulled her into his arms, holding her fast against his solid warmth.

"That's enough," he said gently. "We won't talk about this any more tonight. Come on. We're going to get some sleep."

"You understand?" she asked on a sniffle as he led her inside and pushed the doors closed behind them.

"Of course." He lifted her in his arms and put her in the middle of the downy comforter.

"Thank you," she said, clutching his neck before letting him go. "Thank you. That makes it easier."

Chapter Eleven

It was not until Kellen stood beside Dominic at the stove the following morning, her heart breaking, her hands rock-steady with the control she exerted over herself, that she realized they'd not been speaking the same language the night before.

She turned sizzling bacon in a pan while he flipped eggs to fit the preference of everyone at the table—over well for Rocco, over easy for the boys, sunny-side up for Mary Ellen.

Kellen was remembering the dark, velvet night she'd spent in Dominic's arms, held close and safe and quiet. Their closeness doubled her pain this morning, but she'd added it to her treasure of memories to summon up later as her life went on without him.

Mary Ellen brought her plate and cup to the counter, gave Kellen a kiss on the cheek, then stood on tiptoe to offer one to Dominic. He leaned down with a grin to accommodate her.

"That was a wonderful breakfast," she said. "You're a great team. Got to put my face on."

Dominic served up the boys' seconds, then made a plate for Kellen and joined her at the table. Rocco hand washed the dishes while they ate, scooped theirs away when they were finished and poured them more coffee, then unplugged the pot. Then he glanced at his watch.

"Better get a move on," he said, then disappeared upstairs with the boys.

Dominic went to wash the coffeepot, and Kellen found a dish towel and began to dry the things on the drainboard.

"Leave that," he said, quickening his movements as everyone thundered down the stairs again.

"Come on, Dad," Ethan shouted into the kitchen as he passed on his way to the door. "Uncle Rocco says it's time."

Kellen's heartache seemed to stifle her breath and close her throat. There was so much she wanted to say.

Everyone ran past the kitchen door, her mother included, without stopping to say goodbye. She felt desperate and uncertain, as though she wanted to chase them down and tell them goodbye—but she had Dominic alone for one precious moment and there was something she had to tell him.

He was rolling his shirtsleeves down and smiling gently at her.

"Dominic," she whispered. "I...the way I feel about our relationship doesn't mean I don't love you. I do." She said it again because she needed to. "I love you so much."

"I know," he responded with that same understanding tone he'd used the night before.

Then he scooped her up in his arms and headed for the door. "That's why I'm taking you with me. Flip the light switch."

He stopped at the threshhold. Automatically, she did as he asked and bathed the house in midmorning quiet.

"Now open the door."

He stopped at the door, waiting for her to comply. Temper rose hotly along with undeniable relief.

"Last night you said—"

"I said we wouldn't talk about it anymore," he explained patiently. "I didn't say I'd changed my mind. Turn the knob, please."

"You said you understood."

"I do. You're afraid and just a little crazy. Turn the knob."

With a halfhearted glower at him, she turned the knob. Ethan was there to close and lock the door after them. He winked at his father as he preceded him to the car. "Cool move, Dad. I didn't know you could do this sort of stuff." He looked over his shoulder to indicate Kellen in his father's arms.

A car full of grinning faces welcomed Kellen as Dominic put her into the front seat beside his uncle, climbed in beside her and pulled his door closed.

As they sorted out seat belts, she asked quietly, "So you had everyone on your side, did you?"

He nodded unapologetically. "I did."

"I'll get you for this," she threatened.

"You've already got me," he told her. "I'm just going to work on you until you realize it."

"Dominic..." Her eyes took on that sadness that so plagued him. "This is only going to make it harder when I have to leave."

"When you see our place in Connecticut," he declared confidently, certain it would wipe that look from her eyes once and for all, "you won't want to leave. Now buckle up and be quiet. Rocco likes to sing from *La Traviata* when he drives."

"I'VE NEVER SEEN anything like this," Mary Ellen confided to Kellen in a whisper as they followed behind a liveried driver who led the boys toward a long black limousine visible beyond the terminal's double glass doors. "First class travel with all the perks, greeted by a cheering crowd at the gate and picked up in a limo!"

"The cheering crowd was for Dominic, Mom," Kellen pointed out unnecessarily.

"I know, but wasn't it exciting! It was like arriving with the Dodgers or the Beatles, or something. They were waving the *New York Times* headline about Dominic nailing Mueller."

Kellen rolled her eyes. "I know, Mom. I was there."

Mary Ellen glanced at her and sniffed doubtfully. "Were you, really? I got the distinct impression you were having an out-of-body experience somewhere else. What is wrong with you?"

"You all tricked me, that's what's wrong with me."

Mary Ellen stopped on the sidewalk beyond the doors. They stood in the long shadows of late afternoon.

"Tell me that you're not deliriously happy to be here instead of home alone with Carrot."

Kellen glanced back toward the terminal. "I hope Rocco and Dominic remember to pick her up. She'll be very unhappy that she traveled as freight."

"Don't change the subject. You've been behaving like a wind in a snit all day, but I'm your mother. I know every look in your eyes, and you're in love, Kellen Bedelia.''

"Love has nothing to do with it."

Mary Ellen looked at her as though she were crazy. "Love has everything to do with everything! My God, where did I go wrong? Must be the genes from your father's side."

Kellen followed her mother into the limo, wondering if she had any idea how right she was.

IN THE SOFT LIGHT of a bright blue dusk, Kellen saw that the Hunter home was a two-storied symmetrical structure with a covered porch, three dormer windows, and what appeared to be sunrooms on both sides of the entry area.

"It looks like plantation style, but not quite," Mary Ellen remarked as Dominic helped her out of the limousine while the driver and Rocco dealt with luggage.

"It's called Creole," he replied, reaching in after her to help Kellen out. "Betsy and I picked it out of a book. She wanted something with lots of interesting angles and nooks and crannies, and I wanted something simple and clean."

"You told me once you always get your way," Kellen said as he pushed the door closed behind her.

"In this particular case, it was a matter of economics. Nooks and crannies and interesting angles cost a lot more to build, and I'd just gotten my first six-figure advance. Low six-figures. We wanted to start college funds and have enough left to decorate."

Kellen felt small for having suggested the decision had been a matter of selfishness on his part, when she'd never seen a sign of that fault in him.

"It's beautiful," she said, her tone apologetic. She looked around in the gathering darkness. "The boys told me you have horses and lots of wildflowers in the spring."

Dominic pointed to a stable some distance away beyond a split-rail corral. "Horses. You'll see the flowers about April."

She ignored his reference to her permanent residence and happily took the hand Travis offered to lead her toward the front porch and the white-aproned figure now standing at the top.

At the foot of the stairs, Travis tore away from Kellen to run up into the woman's arms.

"Mrs. Gibbons, you won't believe what's happened to us!" he cried with a dramatic hand to his heart.

"I will!" she corrected, hugging him fiercely. "I read all about it in the paper and your father's agent called."

Ethan, walking past the short, round woman with Carrot in a mesh-domed cat carrier, reached out to hook an arm around her. Carrot protested the jostling with a shrill meow as the carrier tipped slightly.

"Hey, Mrs. Gibbons," he greeted. "We're so glad to be home. I hope you made lace cookies."

"Of course I did, but you leave them alone until after dinner. Is this Carrot?"

Ethan looked surprised. "How'd you know?"

"Your father called me this morning. I put a cat box in the laundry room, so just show her where it is, then let her out of there, poor kitty."

She leaned down to look into the cage and speak nonsense to the cat, who shrank back.

"Right." Ethan hurried off to do as he'd been told.

Dominic, loping up the stairs, caught Kellen's arm and brought her with him. At the top, he hugged the stout woman, then turned her to face Kellen.

"Kellen, this is Pauline Gibbons, our housekeeper and unofficial grandmother. Mrs. Gibbons, this is Kellen Clark who was featured in the news story this morning."

Kellen glanced up at him in surprise. Everyone else in their party had devoured the newspaper account of their adventure, but Kellen felt she'd stored it in her mind just the way she wanted to keep it. "I was?" she asked.

He shook his head over her.

Mrs. Gibbons hugged her tightly, then stepped back to give her a wide, motherly smile. "Welcome. As a reward for your courage and for taking such good care of Mr. Hunter, I'm going to feed you until you burst and see to your every need."

"I'm her mother," Mary Ellen piped up as she climbed the porch steps on Rocco's arm. "Can I command the same treatment for having had the foresight to give birth to her?"

Mrs. Gibbons laughed and hugged her, too. Kellen didn't like the look of that. They seemed like two of a kind already. Outnumbered, and she'd just gotten here.

Mrs. Gibbons smiled a little doubtfully at Rocco. "Mr. Musante. It's nice to see you again."

Rocco bowed deferentially. "And you, Mrs. Gibbons."

Dominic ushered everyone inside, dispatched the boys to help their uncle settle into a room he regularly occupied on his visits, and sent Mrs. Gibbons to make Mary Ellen comfortable in the room across the hall from Rocco.

As Dominic flipped through a thick stack of mail on the coffee table in the living room, Kellen looked around herself in awe.

All the walls were white, and all the plump, country-style furniture was covered with bright fabrics in primary colors, prints and plaids mixed in a cheerfully chaotic combination Kellen admired. Honey oak trimmed the doorways and window frames, provided the large slab of a mantel over the stone fireplace, and wound upward from the edge of the room on the light-carpeted, circular stairway.

Rooms seemed to wander into each other. She saw a big airy kitchen in white and yellow with hanging pots and flourishing plants off one edge of the room. It appeared to open into a dining room with heavy oak table and chairs she could also glimpse, and immediately to her right was a sun room with natural wicker, white shutters, and a baker's rack filled with plants.

Dominic finally dropped the pile of mail back onto the table and took her elbow.

"Nothing that can't wait awhile. Come on. I'll show you to your room."

She gave him a knowing look. "It wouldn't happen to be the same one you occupy, would it?"

"It would," he answered amiably with little sign of guilt. "But in my role as host, I'll let you have my bed and I'll sleep on the sofa in my office."

Kellen felt ambivalent as she let herself be led down a short corridor that opened onto an enormous bedroom. Pique seemed to be uppermost, which didn't surprise her after an entire day of having her every wish thwarted. She was just surprised to find that despite all her protests, she'd been looking forward to sleeping in Dominic's arms.

Here the walls were a soft ivory. The four-poster bed was of light wood with a long, low matching dresser that ran the length of one wall to abut a walk-in wardrobe that was bigger than Kellen's entire bedroom.

A stone fireplace separated the bedroom from the office and warmed both rooms. Though "office" was hardly the word she would use to describe the cozy atmosphere of the book-lined room with its sofa and chair in nubby green and white check, wet bar, and computer center.

"It looks like someone's working living room." She went to sliding doors that looked out onto a roomy deck. A big yellow Labrador looked back at her, tongue lolling, tail wagging furiously.

"Oh!" she said, delighted, and stepped onto the deck.

"Watch your…coat," Dominic called after her, but he was already too late. Big paws left their imprint on her sleeves as she caught the dog against her and leaned down to be kissed.

"Dandy, down!" Dominic ordered sharply. The dog complied immediately—for about five seconds—then forgot and leapt at Kellen again, eager to make a new friend.

Dominic laughed and pulled her away, to be treated immediately to the same extravagant affection. The dog licked his face and ears while whining ecstatically.

"This is Dandelion," he said, making the dog sit and squatting down beside her to scratch her chest. "She's just over a year, but still very much a puppy. Unfortunately she has the strength of a horse, so be careful."

"How does she feel about cats?" Kellen asked.

"She loves everything unconditionally," he replied. "And enthusiastically. She won't hurt Carrot. Our neighbor's cat naps right up against her all the time."

At that moment the boys came out from the other end of the house and the dog ran for them in the near darkness, barking her delight at having them back. Dominic reached inside the room and flipped a switch that lit the back of the house with spotlights.

He watched the boys and the dog roughhouse, a small smile on his lips. "It is so good to be home," he said with quiet sincerity.

Kellen was touched by his tone. She tended to forget, she realized, how much he must have worried about his children while they were separated, how much he must have missed the warmth and comfort of this wonderful place while he was stuck with her in a dark tunnel.

"I'm glad you're all safe and sound," she told him. "That it all worked out."

He turned to look down at her, the gravity in his voice visible in the dark depths of his eyes. "We're all safe and sound, but it hasn't all worked out. Not yet."

She knew he was talking about her. She gave him a quick smile, reluctant to argue and spoil the precious moment for him, but unwilling to let him assume he would get what he wanted simply because he wanted it.

"Sure it has," she teased, walking back inside. He followed her and slid the door closed. "You have me here at your mercy, and added to that—" She turned in the middle of the room to spread both hands out in a gesture of helplessness "—I haven't any clothes. Perfect setup for you."

He went to the wardrobe to pull blankets and a pillow out of the back.

"I'm sleeping on the sofa while you're here," he said with a sidelong glance as he passed her on his way to it. "I forced you to come, but that's all I'll force you to do. I want you to enjoy my home, spend time with my boys, get a real picture of what my life is like before you decide once and for all that you don't want to share it with me."

The truth was, he was hoping if he couldn't prove to her that he was real by being close to her, perhaps he could prove it by keeping his distance. Absence was supposed to make the heart grow fonder, wasn't it?

For Kellen, pique became disappointment, which she kept carefully to herself. To show him that his plan would suit her just fine, she went to the bed, sat on the edge of it and bounced several times.

"I hope you'll be comfortable," she said lightly, as though it were her last concern. "I'm sure I will."

He smiled, his eyes telling her that he doubted she would be. "Dinner's usually at seven, but I can ask Mrs. Gibbons to delay it if you need more time."

"I can freshen up in ten minutes. I have makeup in my purse, but nothing to change into—so it won't take long."

"We'll rectify that tomorrow. I have to do a few things in Hartford, so I'll drop you and your mother off to go shopping. I still have open accounts at a few of the shops Betsy preferred."

She frowned at him and stood off the bed. "I don't like the idea of you buying clothes for me."

He raised an eyebrow.

"And don't tell me," she warned, "that I'd better get used to it."

It had been on the tip of his tongue, but he'd wisely held it back.

"Consider it a loan," he said easily. "If you don't stay, you can repay me when you get back to Sandpiper."

She thought about what it would be like to return to Sandpiper without him. The thought took the form of a long black hole, a little like the tunnel at the battery, only without him to warm her, to make her laugh, to make her love. As the feeling of emptiness filled her heart, she turned away from him, smoothing the bedspread she'd disturbed.

"Deal," she agreed. "Now, if you'll give me a few minutes, I'll try to do the best I can with what I'm wearing."

Controlled, she turned back to him and gave him a theatrical curtsy in her old navy sweats.

It would be fine with him if she never wore anything else, he thought. The stark simplicity of the dark color and simple lines only exaggerated the grace of a face and form that had grown more beautiful to him with each moment he spent in her company.

But he preferred her hair loose. On the airplane, she'd gone into the ladies' room and returned with her hair brushed and tied at the nape of her neck with a simple scrap of red ribbon she'd found in her purse, a remnant of one of the windows she'd decorated.

Unable to stop the action, he crossed the space between them and reached behind her to give the tail of the bow a yank. Her hair fell free, long and lustrous and shimmering with red highlights, one long wave settling over her left eye.

The urge to brush it back and kiss her was almost overwhelming. But it would defeat his purpose in sleeping on the sofa, and keeping her here forever was more important to him than having her now, at this moment.

"You should find everything you need." He pointed to the bathroom at the near end of the office. "But if you're lacking anything, just press the intercom and Mrs. Gibbons will pick up."

"Right." The word came out soft and high. She had gooseflesh on her neck where his hand had brushed her to untie her ribbon. Desire burned in her like a wound.

When he was gone, Kellen stood under a hot shower in a stall that could accommodate two. She prayed for the ability to hold out against what she wanted in favor of what she knew to be best.

"Please, God," she whispered as water drummed on her shoulders. "Don't let me live my mother's life over again."

Chapter Twelve

An empty dining room greeted Kellen when she went down to dinner. The table was set with china and silver, a wine carafe stood in the middle, and two glasses of milk had been poured.

Checking the kitchen, Kellen found it filled with a wonderful, spicy aroma, but no people. Then the sound of excited conversation came from a room at the far end.

She went to investigate, and found a large laundry room that also accommodated an ironing board, a sewing machine, a desk and a sorting table, filled with every member of the household.

Ethan and Travis were on their knees in front of the desk, with everyone else leaning over them.

"Bring her a shrimp from the cocktails."

"Have you tried a saucer of milk?"

"Leave her alone. She'll come out on her own."

Carrot. Kellen squeezed between her mother and Uncle Rocco to get to the desk under which her cat was apparently hiding.

"She's frightened," Mrs. Gibbons said sympathetically, stepping aside to let her through. "She was sitting in here on the dryer, and Dandy came in and scared her to death.''

Travis looked up. ''Dandy just wanted to be friends, but Carrot got scared. We put the dog back outside.''

Ethan moved aside to make room for Kellen as she got down on her knees. She had to literally double over to see into the narrow space between the short legs of the desk and the white linoleum. Carrot had somehow wedged herself into the small space between the kneehole and the side of the desk and did not look prepared to move.

Kellen reached a hand in, thinking that her familiar scent might calm her. Instead, Carrot hissed, clawed her, and retreated as far to the back as her confining space would allow.

Kellen drew back a hand with three stinging stripes on it and sat back on her heels, wondering what to do.

''I think we should just leave her alone,'' Dominic said reasonably, ''and she'll come out when she's ready.''

''But she's so scared, Dad,'' Travis said.

Rocco, accustomed to action, suggested, ''Why don't we just pick up the desk? Dom, take that side.''

''No,'' Dominic said. ''Leave her alone. She'll come out when she's—''

''She'll starve, Dad,'' Travis pleaded.

''Dominic,'' Rocco said forcefully, his voice deepening like that of a baritone taking center stage. He pointed to the other side of the desk. ''Is that the way to talk to the uncle who saved your life? Take that side of the desk!''

''You did not save my life,'' Dominic retorted as he lifted. ''Kellen and the boys did.''

"But I arrived in the nick of time."

"You were late."

As the desk rose off the floor, a flash of orange flew through arms and legs as though turbo-charged and disappeared into the kitchen. From their vantage point in the laundry room, everyone saw Carrot leap onto the dishwasher and disappear down the back of it.

Mrs. Gibbons gasped. "There isn't but four inches of space back there."

Everyone groaned.

"Well, that was a good move, Unc," Dominic said dryly as they put the desk down. "Got her out from under the desk all right."

Rocco jabbed a good-natured finger into his nephew's shoulder. "'Leave her alone.' What kind of a solution is that?"

"It ceases to be a problem for us," Dominic explained, "and lets the cat solve it for herself. Which she's perfectly capable of doing when she's ready."

Rocco shook his head at Dominic, his expression heavy with concern. "You'd never run the south side of Chicago, my boy."

Dominic nodded. "That's good because I have enough trouble with this little corner of Connecticut. Can we eat now? Everyone agreed, the cat will come out when it's ready? Kellen?"

Kellen nodded, remembering that Carrot once hid for three days in the bottom of her closet when she'd had a new water heater installed.

"Carrot's just not very brave," she said. "She'll come out when she's hungry."

"What does she like best?" Mrs. Gibbons asked, stopping at the stove as everyone else streamed through the kitchen toward the dining room.

"Chicken," Kellen replied. "White meat."

"I'll put some out."

KELLEN HAD NEVER eaten so much, nor felt so exhausted. Filled with succulent chicken divan and homemade rolls, she tried to refuse chocolate cake, but was coaxed by Rocco who claimed to have had a hand in its preparation. When she resisted further, he fed her a bite. After one taste of the mocha flavor, she ate the rest on her own, grateful that her sweats could expand several inches.

"You wearing down?" Dominic asked, when everyone dispersed from the table, Rocco and Mary Ellen to have a game of chess, the boys to get ready for school the next day.

"I guess it's finally catching up with me," she admitted, putting a hand to her woozy head. "I feel as though I could sleep for twelve hours."

"Come on," he said, putting an arm around her shoulders and leading her across the dark living room toward the bedroom. "I'll make sure you have everything you need. What about pajamas?"

She allowed herself the luxury of leaning against him. "I sleep in the buff."

"Mmm. Well, that'll be a delicious thought to keep me awake tonight. I'll leave a night-light on so you don't wander the wrong way when you get up for a glass of water."

"You wouldn't like it?" she teased drowsily.

"I would." He guided her toward the bed. Her eyes were almost closed now. "But I want you clear-headed enough to decide to marry me, and I know how you are when I make love to you."

"I lost...my head over...over you," she said around a yawn as she collided with the mattress. "Just like a fairy-tale...maiden."

Dominic supported her with one arm while yanking the covers back with the other. Then he sat her on the edge of the bed, raised her arms, then raised them again when they immediately flopped down. He held her wrists above her head in one hand, then eased the sweatshirt up with the other.

"What're you doing?" she asked with distinct lack of interest, her eyes completely closed.

"You said you sleep in the buff," he said. "I just want you to be comfortable."

He tugged the sweatshirt up, then released her wrists to yank it up and off. She immediately fell toward him, her cheek against his waist.

He leaned down to kiss the top of her head, then unhooked her bra, lay her back against the pillows, then tossed the bra aside. He groaned quietly but painfully at the sight of her and the knowledge that he'd be sleeping on the sofa.

He tugged the bottoms and her panties down in one swift sweep, glancing once at the slender line of her, every inch of which he knew in intimate detail and now longed for with every breath of life in him.

He yanked the blankets up to her chin to save himself further frustration. This was the right thing to do. It would pay off for him in the end. He was strong enough to do this. Yeah, right.

KELLEN ENCOUNTERED a strange sight in the kitchen the following morning. As the boys raced past her, shouting their goodbyes, schoolbooks under their arms, she went to take her place between her mother, who was engrossed in the morning paper, and Dominic, who was talking to Rocco.

But she couldn't get to the chair. Something large and yellow with an appendage that was swinging like a metronome had its head stuck under it. From somewhere underneath, in the confusion of chair legs and cross pieces, came a very ill-tempered cry. Carrot resisted Dandelion's overtures of friendship.

"Dandy, come!" Dominic called.

She complied immediately, upending the chair and sending the cat back to his spot under the desk in the laundry room. Holding the dog by the collar, Dominic tugged her toward the door.

Mrs. Gibbons, bringing Kellen a plate of still-sizzling bacon and eggs, shook her head over the cat.

"Don't worry, Miss Clark," she said. "I got her to eat half an egg and a piece of bacon under the table before Mr. Hunter and Dandy came back from their jog. She won't starve, but she's certainly going to get lonely."

Mary Ellen looked up from her paper. "Fraidy cats deserve to be lonely." She smiled at her daughter. "Good morning, sweetie."

Kellen, aware of the double entendre in her mother's casual remark, refused to be baited. "Good morning, Mom. Sleep well?"

"Yes. You?"

"Very well." Her reply was bright, a little too bright. She had drifted out of sleep in the middle of the night, vaguely aware of a subtle lack of comfort, of something missing. She'd grown accustomed in the previous two nights to waking up curled against Dominic.

Not fully awake, her subconscious still caught in the dark tunnel that had occupied her dreams, she had reached beside her, found the space empty, then sat up and called Dominic's name.

"Yes?" he'd replied out of the dark.

Still disoriented, she'd asked, confused, "Where are you?"

She'd heard something subtle in his voice. Amusement? Smugness?

"On the sofa, remember?"

"Oh." She'd pulled the blankets up to her chin, embarrassed, and lay back against the pillows. "Yeah. Sorry I woke you."

"I'm not." She'd thought the words implied he'd gained a certain satisfaction out of knowing her first thought on awakening had been to notice and be upset by his absence.

Dominic, resuming his chair, studied her with a suspiciously bland smile.

"Eat up," he coaxed. "We're going to drop Uncle Rocco off at the airport before I leave you at the mall."

Rocco glanced at his watch and pushed his chair back. "I'd better make a few calls and get a move on."

In the past few days Kellen had come to appreciate Rocco's take-charge manner because it encompassed every last person within his perimeter. He was kind and solicitous, though completely unaware of the democratic concept of shared decision making, and unfailingly cheerful. He doted on the boys, flattered Mrs. Gibbons, flirted with Mary Ellen and obviously loved his nephew a great deal.

Kellen raised her steaming cup of coffee to him as he passed her chair. "I'm going to miss you, Rocco. I wish you were *my* uncle."

Rocco stopped and leaned down to wrap an arm around her shoulders and squeeze. "Word is I'm going to be." Then he left the room.

Kellen turned an accusing glance on Dominic.

"What?" he asked in dramatic innocence. "Did I say anything? Mary Ellen, did you hear me say anything?"

Mary Ellen, pretending to be engrossed in the paper but wearing a little smile that said otherwise, shook her head without looking up.

"I didn't hear you say anything, Dom. My goodness! Will you look at this, Kellen! Stirrup pants are two for the price of one at Willoughby's."

Mary Ellen shoved the newspaper ad at Kellen, effectively blocking her view of Dominic and any need to refute his claim of innocence. Kellen let the matter drop. She was sure another opportunity would present itself.

"Mom, it's a beautiful outfit," Kellen said, studying her reflection in the white mohair sweater and white knit stirrup pants her mother had bullied her into trying on. "But I won't buy it."

"Kell—" Mary Ellen began in exasperation.

"Mom." Kellen turned away from the mirror. "First of all, it's almost as much as my van payment, and secondly, where would I ever go to wear this? I mean, white! You know how long this would last with me crawling around in a store window?''

Mary Ellen turned to a plump but pretty young clerk who'd patiently endured their bickering most of the afternoon. "Doesn't this just break your heart?" she asked. "A young woman supposedly in the prime of her intelligence and femininity, and she doesn't know what to do with an outfit that makes the most of her every curve."

The clerk shook her head in complete agreement. "Sad. Would you like to see something in blue polyester?"

At Kellen's dark look, she laughed and approached the mirror to further smooth the lines of the sweater. It had a soft round neck, a subtle silk-embroidery pattern also in white that dipped to a V between her breasts to accentuate them, then swirled back up to the shoulder. The pants tugged in a straight, clingy line over every lean inch of her to disappear inside a pair of low white shoes Mary Ellen had run to the shoe department for to complete the outfit.

"This will stop any man dead and make him roll over for you," she said softly, turning her back to the mirror and studying her reflection from over Kellen's shoulder. "Not only does it cling in the right places, but it makes you look like something an angel might have brought, all soft and sweet and begging to be touched."

"It's just a sweater," Kellen said, denying all its magical properties—until she saw Dominic in the mirror, coming toward them.

In a three-piece gray pin-striped suit, he walked through the lingerie department with complete ease, attracting stares as he passed, bringing women out into the aisles to watch him.

Then he saw Kellen's reflection in the mirror and stopped. His eyes met hers and said everything the clerk had told her a man would feel.

"Don't tell me," the clerk whispered as she moved away, "that Peggy doesn't know her stuff."

Dominic continued toward her at a slower pace, and she became aware of everyone watching. He didn't stop until he was right behind her, and then it was only to turn her into his arms. He looked down at her with all the need she'd felt the night before when she'd awakened and found herself alone in his bed.

Then he wove his hand into her hair, gently tugged her head back and kissed her, that same desperate need in his lips and in the hand splayed between her shoulder blades holding her to him.

It went on interminably, bold and delicious and dismayingly possessive.

When he finally raised his head there was a communal scream of delight and appreciative applause from their audience.

"Don't grump at me," he said with a quiet grin. "The reaction was beyond my control."

"She'll take that outfit in every color," Mary Ellen said, a finger raised to claim Peggy's attention. "And do you have it in my size?"

DOMINIC WANDERED out of his office late that night, hoping a cup of cappuccino would revive him for the hour or so he still had to put in at the computer. He knew Kellen hadn't gone to bed, but he'd thought she was playing Balderdash with her mother and Mrs. Gibbons in the family room.

He was surprised when he heard her voice coming from the laundry room.

"This is silly, you know, and completely counter-productive," she was saying. "The more you try to avoid the inevitable, the more you'll be pursued. And the more you're pursued, the harder it'll be for you to turn around and face it."

Frowning to himself, he followed the sound. Was she arguing with herself?

He rounded the corner into the room to find her lying on the floor on her stomach in a pair of graphite-colored tights she'd bought that afternoon, and a hunter green sweatshirt. The long shirt had hiked up to her waist at some point in her conversation with Carrot, and the sight of her bottom snugly wrapped in graphite knit made his breath catch—and did a few other things to him he found it safer not to consider.

Her toes in laceless black tennies were braced against the linoleum, her head turned so that her cheek was against the floor as she peered under the desk.

"I know you didn't have dinner tonight," she said softly, coaxingly. She pushed a saucer of pungent-smelling cat food under the desk. "Wouldn't you like to come out and eat? That's it . . . a little closer . . ."

Hastily, she withdrew the saucer. A white-tipped orange paw came out in pursuit of it and Kellen caught it.

"Gotcha! Come out of there you little wimp. Dandy's upstairs in Ethan's room and it's time you— Ouch!"

Dominic went forward as she sat up on her knees, putting the palm of her hand to her mouth with a disgruntled groan. He reached under her arms and pulled her up.

"I thought we'd decided to wait it out until Carrot surfaces on her own. Let me see that."

She held out a small palm with three livid scratches on it to match the ones on the back of her hand. He led her into the tiny bathroom off the utility room.

"That was your suggestion," she said with a sigh. "I don't think it's going to work."

"You haven't given it time."

"The way it's going," she said as he pulled a tube of ointment out of the medicine cabinet, "I'm going to have to go home without her, and you're going to live the rest of your natural life with a cat somewhere under your furniture."

He rolled his eyes at her exaggeration. "Wash your hands, please."

She did, then eyed him wryly as she dried them on a blue hand towel.

"You're not going to say, 'Kellen, you know you're never leaving here'?" she asked.

He ignored her question, turning her palm up in one hand while he applied antiseptic with the other. "You know, you remind me a lot of Carrot."

"Really? How so?"

"Several ways." He capped the tube and put it away. Then without warning, he put a hand to her back and pulled her close until she was sharply aware of every cell of their bodies in contact. She held her oily hand away from him, everything inside her that moved picking up speed.

He ran a hand lightly down her spinal column to its very base, then slowly, long fingers pressed against her hips, stroking upward.

She gasped a little moan of sound.

"You purr," he said.

She tore her concentration away from his touch to give him a scolding look.

"You scratch," he went on. "And you hide under the furniture of your past to avoid having to confront the fact that you love me."

She pushed lightly against him. "I told you I love you."

He held firm. "But love is a lot more than words. You have to show it."

Her eyes, now wide and limpid from his touch, challenged him with a direct look. "You're saying I haven't shown you that I love you?"

"You've made love with me," he said, his voice deepening a little at the memories the words evoked. Then he added on a little laugh, "Divinely. But contrary to society's attitude today, you don't just coast with love for as long as it serves your purpose. You take action with it, you make decisions because of it, you take chances, and build dreams, and do brave and noble things."

"Or you get divorced." She pushed against him once more, her eyes brimming, her jaw set, and he freed her, tempted to swat her for her stubbornness as she walked away.

With the toe of his shoe, he nudged the saucer of cat food under the desk. Someone may as well face the long night satisfied.

THANKSGIVING DAY was cold and bleak, snow flurries drifting in the sharp wind like fairy dust. With Mrs. Gibbons celebrating with her family, everyone helped put the bird in the oven and prepare the trimmings for further attention later in the afternoon.

Mary Ellen, munching chips and dip in front of the television, stayed to mind the kitchen while Dominic and Kellen and the boys took a long walk off their property and down the road, around a small lake where mallards and loons swam in picturesque contentment.

Snow clouds were low and heavy, the tall conifers that surrounded the lake losing their pointed tops among them. Colorful little boats were moored at intervals from docks that fronted the homes that populated the lakefront.

There were several old Victorians, a few starkly modern homes and several small cabins with smoke puffing from their chimneys.

"Mom used to come here all the time," Ethan said, picking up a pebble and tossing it expertly so that it skipped across the glasslike surface of the water.

Kellen noticed that she heard no grief in his voice, just a comfortable sound as though the thought of her there was a pleasant memory for him.

"I can see why," she said. "It's breathtakingly beautiful, but it isn't lonely."

Dandelion barked at something in the trees up ahead and ran off in that direction. The boys followed her, Travis trying manfully to keep up with Ethan's longer stride.

"Do you worry about being lonely?" Dominic asked as they followed along at a slower pace, his arm around her shoulders.

"No," she replied, then amended truthfully, "that is, I don't... ordinarily."

"But you do now."

It wasn't a question. He knew it to be fact. And he was right. After all they'd been through together, after having talked to him, eaten with him, run with him, made love with him, she knew she was no longer the same woman Spike and Gordy had kidnapped.

She was someone else. A woman whose being had been fused with his, emotionally and physically, and life without him would deprive her of something very vital to a healthy existence.

"Yes," she said.

He held her closer to him as they continued to walk. "You don't think it'd be wiser to stay with us on the fifty-fifty chance what happened to your parents won't happen to us?"

She leaned into him, feeling serious pain because she'd spent several days now with his children, in his home, and she knew very specifically what she couldn't have.

"The odds aren't that good," she answered, "because that was one hundred percent of my life. I know how real the threat is."

He shook his head, his voice for the first time since she'd known him taking on a genuinely grim note.

"Interesting," he said, "that you don't consider what we feel for each other real, yet something that certainly affected you but happened to two other people almost twenty years ago is the most real thing in your life and has served to cut off so many of your options."

"Look!" Travis shouted as he and Ethan emerged from the trees, Dandy tied to the leash Ethan carried. He was pointing to the sky. "Geese!"

Kellen tipped her head back, bumping against Dominic's shoulder. Against the pewter sky was a long, irregular V of geese pointed south. The busy, conversational sound of their honking carried clearly on the cold air.

It represented for Kellen the poignancy of fall—things changing, the passing of the "easy" season, moving on to continue in a warmer, more comfortable place.

Two voices battled inside her, suggesting it was time she made such a move. One told her she could only do that safely by going home. The other said that could only be accomplished here. And for the first time in her life that she could remember, she truly didn't know what to do.

If she stayed and things didn't work out between her and Dominic, she would have hurt everyone. If she went home, she would still hurt everyone.

She stopped walking, momentarily overwhelmed by confusion.

Dominic looked down into her eyes and caught the first glimmer of hope on his horizon. She didn't look quite so sure of herself anymore. In fact, she looked downright befuddled. He pretended not to notice, carefully casual as he tugged the bright red stocking cap lower over her ears.

"Tickle fight!" Travis shouted.

Dominic groaned softly. "Oh, no."

"What?" Kellen asked, distracted from her confusing thoughts.

At that moment the boys came running toward them full tilt, the dog racing along beside them, barking with excitement.

She put her hand on Dominic's arm, uttering a startled laugh. "What's happening?"

"Tickle fight," he warned, pulling her down to her knees, wrapping his arms around her. "Curl against me. Make yourself as small a target as you can."

Dominic turned his back to Dandy as she struck them first, colliding with him with a joyous bark, taking his ear in her mouth and nibbling. Then Ethan hit, his strong body, rolling them over. Travis landed on top, shouting and already laughing hysterically.

Kellen screamed, then joined in the laughter as Travis and Dandy worked her over. Dominic contended with Ethan, noting with a kind of painful pride that he was gaining strength and learning how to use it. He was on the road to manhood.

Just when the notion was beginning to depress Dominic, Ethan gave in and sagged against him, breathing heavily and still laughing.

"Yo, Dad!" he said, laughing as he gulped for air. "We haven't had this much fun since...in a long time."

Dominic guessed what he'd been about to say. "Since Mom died." Kellen apparently guessed it, too, because she looked up at him. She held a giggling Travis in the crook of her arm in an awkward half-nelson, and he thought he saw pleasure in her eyes.

"WHAT DO YOU MEAN, go to New York?" Ethan protested over a mouthful of turkey leg. "We just got home."

"I know," Dominic explained patiently, "but I have to see my publisher and talk over the changes that'll be involved in my book. It'll only take a couple of days."

Kellen stared in surprise, wondering why he hadn't mentioned the trip. Then she realized she had no right to expect to be privy to such information. She'd told him over and over again that she wasn't staying.

"Will Kellen get to stay?" Travis asked.

It would be easier for both of them, for her to leave while he was gone, she thought. But Travis looked so hopeful, so anxious for her to stay.

Dominic nodded. "Kellen's staying."

They shared one stubborn glance across the table, neither looking away, until Mary Ellen patted Kellen's arm with more force than necessary and asked her to pass the gravy.

Chapter Thirteen

Dominic checked the sleeping boys, checked the locks and windows, turned on the security system and walked through the quiet house, turning off lights as he went.

There was a hum inside him, a need for Kellen that was not going to be subdued tonight. He justified changing his plan to make her need him by telling himself this was part of a new plan, a more clever ruse she would not expect.

He turned off the hall light, opened the door quietly and knew the moment he stepped inside the room that she was still awake.

"Can't sleep?" he asked, pushing the door closed.

It was a moment before she answered. "I didn't want to," she said softly.

He went toward the bed in the darkness, drawn like a receptor to a signal.

He sat on the edge of the mattress and saw as his eyes adjusted to the dark that she sat propped up against the pillows. The blankets were pulled up to her breasts, but her shoulders were bare. The hum inside him seemed to stretch and grow.

"I thought you came to bed because you were dead on your feet?" he asked.

"I came to bed," she corrected with a little sigh, "because I couldn't stand to sit beside you on the sofa another moment without wrapping my arms around you."

The hum became a buzz. He had to concentrate to think around it.

"You weren't thinking I'd have complained."

"No." There was wry humor in her voice. "I just didn't want to make things any harder for us than they already are. I'll have to leave when you get back, you know."

He knew that was what she'd been thinking. It served to further justify employment of the new plan.

"I know," he replied, injecting his voice with understanding.

Kellen felt a sense of disappointment that he accepted the fact so easily, but a sense of relief, too, that he'd finally stopped fighting her on it.

"Then I got to thinking," she continued, holding the covers to her breast as she sat forward, within touching distance. She could see the stormy darkness of his eyes in the shadows, the comforting width of his shoulders. For a moment she was immersed in memories of their time in the tunnel—how dark their surroundings had been, how light she'd felt inside herself.

She put a hand to his shoulder and stroked gently.

"That would make this our last night together," she said, her voice barely audible. "Wouldn't it be foolish for me to spend it in your bed while you're on the sofa?"

She couldn't be making this easier for him if she'd tried—or maybe it would ultimately make things more difficult. Whatever happened, he was a man who took his best chance, however dangerous it was.

His answer was immediate and nonverbal. He pulled her out from under the covers and into his lap, his hands stroking, shaping, teasing as he kissed her with all the release of the banked frustration of the last few days and nights.

She unbuttoned his shirt while she kissed him back, pushing it back off his shoulders, then drawing away only to pull his T-shirt up and off. She kissed the line of his shoulder, up his neck, along his jaw, and came back to his mouth with flattering hunger. It was clear the distance he'd kept since he'd brought her home had been no easier on her than him.

She knelt astride him and pushed him back against the mattress, running a line of kisses from his clavicle down to his belt as she unbuckled it. She unzipped his pants, slipped her fingers in the waistband of his briefs.

He braced up on his elbows to allow her to pull them off, the gentle scrape of her fingernails along his thighs as she did so a memory he knew would live with him a long, long time.

But if he was to make this night so memorable she'd be miserable without him, he had to wrest control and soon. In another moment he'd no longer have the resolution to do it.

He rolled them over, catching her wrists when she tried to touch him. He eased her up to the pillow and placed each of her hands under it.

"You have to leave them there," he said, planting a kiss in the hollow of her throat. "Or I'm going to stop."

"What?" she demanded in a disbelieving whisper.

"Don't move your hands from under the pillow," he said, nibbling lightly where he had just kissed. "Or I'll go back to the sofa."

"Dominic! What..."

"This was your idea," he reminded mildly. "You lured me into this. You have to do it my way."

She raised her head off the pillow, but he noted with satisfaction that she hadn't moved her hands.

"Oh, right. Like you fought me so hard. Lovemaking is supposed to take two."

"You'll have your chance to participate later," he told her, pushing her head back to the pillow with a kiss. "For now, do as I say."

She did. Kellen lay, unmoving, while he placed one hand under her back and the other under her hips and raised her waist ever so slightly off the mattress, just enough that her body was arched over his hands, her head falling back, her breasts and her throat offered to him. He smiled to himself when she clutched the pillow in her hands to keep them there.

He kissed her abdomen, then dotted kisses randomly up her body, over the little rise of her rib cage, then over each breast, pausing to tease each with his tongue and his teeth.

She moaned, arching even farther, taking a fistful of his hair in one hand. Then remembering, she put her hand back to the pillow, promising that her retribution would be slow and thorough.

He made a sound of anticipation and now dropped kisses down her body, finally placing her back against the mattress and tipping her hips up.

Kellen felt like some sophisticated explosive device, ticking frantically, energy building toward an inevitable conclusion. But the inevitable danced just out of her reach.

She braced for it, reached toward it, but Dominic held it away, driving her to the very edge of madness, then bringing her back just to do it over again.

Trembling with her need of him, every heightened little sense within her screaming, she finally tossed the pillow, took two handsfuls of his hair and tugged until he raised his body over hers in one smooth stretch.

"I want you, Dominic," she said in a tone that was breathless but brooked no argument.

His white grin shone in the darkness. "That's all I wanted to hear."

Then he was inside her, and she felt one small instant's relief at the knowledge that now, surely... But he drew the madness out even further, turning the bed, the blanket she clutched, the very air she breathed into one quaking, waiting agony.

He couldn't withhold himself another moment. She was desperate and he was worse. He went even more deeply into her, as though reaching for something that would hold this night and all she meant to him alive in her mind, something that wouldn't ever let her forget one sensory impression of it for as long as she lived.

He felt her quake and close around him even tighter as he experienced his own release like so much light and fire passed between them. They shook with it for long moments, clinging together, her arms now wrapped around him as she wept softly into his shoulder.

ICY WIND AND SLEET whipped against the windows all day Saturday. Kellen took a long morning walk while the boys continued to sleep, heading for the spot Ethan had told her his mother used to love.

Today the view was less than rustic calendar quality. Early winter fog hung low over the lake, shrouding the view of the boats and homes and chimneys that were probably cheerfully puffing smoke on the opposite shore.

Dominic had left yesterday, and the world seemed to have closed up. Her view of it was confined to a little strip of lake on which one solitary duck sat, seeming to go nowhere. Kellen identified with it immediately, feeling aimless and alone and very, very cold.

She dug her hands into her pockets and hunched farther into the raised collar of her coat, determined that the mood would pass. She'd confronted countless gloomy days in Sandpiper and never been affected this way. In fact, she'd found the moody weather atmospheric rather than depressing, its somnolent sights and sounds calming.

She walked on, thinking she simply needed more oxygen to her brain. She was suffering some kind of chemical imbalance due to... to being three thousand miles from home and without the stabilizing effects of a regular routine.

She stopped half a mile later at the other end of the lake, winded and frozen. She studied the fog inching closer, and tried to spot the duck on what she could see of the lake. But he'd either been enveloped by the fog, or had taken shelter among the reeds on the bank.

Depression closed around her like a fist. She closed her eyes, feeling the biting wind against her face, and tried to imagine that time had stopped and she still lay in Dominic's arms in the early hours of yesterday morning.

She wrapped her arms around herself as warmth stole over her at the memory of all they'd shared. They'd made love again and again and he'd assumed control until the last time, when she'd insisted and he'd let her. She'd spared no effort or ingenuity to drive him as wild as he'd made her, and when they'd finally collapsed together, arms and legs entangled, she'd looked into his face and seen a bittersweet smile. She wondered even now what it had meant.

In THE BACK of a limo somewhere in Manhattan, Dominic stared moodily at the passing scene—tall buildings, rushing people, street vendors—and felt longing for his home and his family burn his gut like an ulcer.

He'd been waiting since yesterday afternoon for the excitement to strike, as it always did when he visited New York. Though he preferred to be home, the pulse of the city invariably raised his own. As a writer in a reportorial genre, he never missed even a subtle detail of his environment, nor failed to be touched by it in some way.

But today he felt like a padded wall. Everything bounced off him, leaving him unaffected. The only thing that moved him was the memory of Kellen in his arms Thanksgiving night.

He tried to block the thought from taking him over as he'd done unsuccessfully for the past twenty-four hours. But again it assumed control of him as she had done, moving across his mind in the sensual detail of slow-motion.

He saw her ivory limbs in the darkness, legs gracefully folded on either side of him, arms moving with balletic perfection, breasts silky and firm to his touch. He saw the undulation of her hair, lustrous even in the dark, as she arched over him with a cry that still rang in his ears. He saw that mass of dark hair fall forward over her face in ripples as she collapsed against him, then felt it cover his face like a skein of silk as she dropped her head beside his on the pillow and nuzzled his ear.

He'd dreamed it all over again last night in his hotel room and now felt her against him so strongly that he thought it was entirely possible the men and women assembled for International Publishing's publicity meeting would be able to see Kellen, hauntingly beautiful in her nakedness, arms and legs wrapped around him.

"God," he said aloud, straightening in his seat, retrieving the outline he'd prepared from his briefcase. He had to get himself together.

The driver lowered the privacy window. "You say something, Mr. Hunter?"

Dominic sighed and smiled. "I was just praying, Parker."

Parker grinned at him in the mirror. "Always a good idea in New York, Mr. Hunter."

KELLEN WAS HALFWAY back to the house when the boys intercepted her.

"Something wrong?" she asked anxiously, wondering if there'd been some problem while she'd been gone.

"No." Travis hooked an arm in hers and walked along beside her.

She looked expectantly from one boy to the other, still convinced they'd come after her for a reason.

Ethan fell into step on her other side, giving her a halfhearted smile, kicking desultorily at a pile of fallen maple leaves.

She put an arm around him, sensing mild distress.

"You sure nothing's wrong?"

To her surprise, he came closer and slipped an arm around the back of her waist. "Well...nothing real," he said after a moment's thought.

Real, she thought dryly. So she wasn't the only one finding the unreal troublesome.

She squeezed his shoulder. "Well, what's the problem that *isn't* real?"

He shrugged. "I don't know. I just wish Dad hadn't had to go to New York so soon after we got home."

"Yeah," Travis chimed in. "Now we have to worry about him all the time."

Kellen frowned down at him. "What do you mean? Mueller is in jail, you know that."

Ethan looked down at his feet as he walked along, as though reluctant to admit his fears to her. "I know. It's just that I never used to think about it. I mean, he'd go off on some trip or other and we'd just wait for him to come home. I never really thought about something happening to him." He looked up at her, his eyes wide and earnest and troubled. "Now I do."

"We used to think he was...like..." Travis thought over an appropriate comparison and finally said, "like Batman, you know. Like he could lick anybody."

Kellen put her arm around him to bring him closer, surprised to find herself reassuring him in a way she wasn't sure was healthy in the long run, but that he seemed to need at the moment.

"Your father is very tall and very strong," she said. "Remember how he punched out Mueller and the man who touched your head?"

Travis nodded. "Yeah. But lots of other stuff can happen. He could be hit by a car, or his plane could crash, or he could get sick."

Like their mother had. Kellen thought she understood the problem—that a serious brush with danger and possible death had given them a new perspective on their father's and probably their own mortality. And he must seem even more vulnerable to them after their mother's death.

"Well, you know," she said carefully, "every one on this earth faces the same danger. That's a chance we all take just to be alive."

"'Cause everybody dies...I mean, sometime," Ethan said.

"Right. But very few people die young, or in the kinds of accidents you're talking about. And the odds are, since your dad has had this happen to him and survived, he'll live to be very old and even to see *your* children."

Ethan brightened a little. "You think so?"

"Yes, I do."

"Are you gonna have children?" Travis asked.

Relieved that he was smiling, Kellen kissed the top of his head. "No, I'm just going to borrow the two of you."

Arm in arm, the three of them turned off the road to the walk that led to the house.

"You can have us full-time if you want," Travis said. "You fit Rule Number One, too."

Kellen looked from one to the other as they marched along. "All right, what is Rule Number One? Even your dad doesn't know what it is."

Ethan smiled. "You have to love Dad as much as Mom did. Easy."

"Right," she said after a startled moment. "Easy."

Mary Ellen, standing at the window with a cup of coffee, moved to open the kitchen door for them as they approached. Her eyes lingered over their companionable posture before they broke ranks to walk up the steps. She raised an eyebrow at Kellen as she held the door for her.

"Don't start with me, Mom," Kellen warned.

"I wish we could do something fun," Travis said as he peeled off his coat.

Mrs. Gibbons brought cups of cocoa to the table and muffins still steaming from the oven.

"You could clean your room," she suggested with a grin.

Travis gave her the half amused, half indignant glance the remark deserved. "I said something *fun*."

Kellen, confused, disturbed, emotionally upended, decided a project would be good for all of them. And a project she knew something about could be particularly productive.

"Do you guys know where the Christmas decorations are?" she asked, pulling off her own coat and putting it on the back of a kitchen chair.

"In the garage somewhere," Ethan answered. "Why?"

"I thought we could get the house all ready for Christmas and surprise your father when he gets back."

Ethan looked interested. Travis was enthused. Then he frowned. "But we always go out together to buy the tree."

She nodded. "We'll do everything but the tree. We'll decorate the stairway and the mantel and his office."

"All *right!*" As they all sat down to cocoa and muffins, Kellen saw her mother catch the housekeeper's eye and wink.

As THOUGH PROVIDED by a Hollywood propman, snow drifted down that afternoon as Kellen and the boys collected holly and evergreen branches. Fat flakes streamed around them as they piled the greens in a wheelbarrow and laughed their way back to the garage struggling to keep the wheelbarrow in an even line. The ground was already growing slippery, Kellen noted, and she wondered how long the snow would last.

They made garlands for the stairway and tied them on at intervals with strips of calico Mrs. Gibbons provided from a box of fabric scraps.

Kellen hung plain red ornaments from the loops of the garland, then stood back with the boys to admire their work.

Travis was wide-eyed. "It's beautiful," he whispered.

Ethan nodded and grinned at her. "Cool," he said.

They filled an empty painted vase on the hearth with holly and draped the mantel with a garland and placed the Nativity figures on it.

In one of the boxes, Kellen found a dilapidated wreath made with silk and dried flowers.

"Mom used to put that on their bedroom door," Ethan said. "But Dad hasn't used it in a couple of years."

"Well." Now into the spirit of the project, Kellen's mind worked swiftly. The wreath had been formed on a straw circle, and she pulled out everything that had become misshapen in the box, or that had disintegrated, and fitted fresh greens around it. She left the boys to add the cones and pods that were still in good condition while she made another bow from Mrs. Gibbons's box. Then they hung the wreath on the door of Dominic's bedroom/office.

Ethan sighed and nodded. "Looks good. I think he'll like it."

On Sunday, while it continued to snow, they hung the outdoor lights with Mrs. Gibbons directing and Mary Ellen alternately shouting instructions and covering her eyes. Ethan's style was to reach as far sideways off the ladder as he could before moving it.

Kellen suggested twice that he step down and move the ladder, but he insisted he was able to reach.

The third time Ethan flailed the air for a heartstopping moment as the ladder wobbled and Mrs. Gibbons hurried with a scream to steady it.

Kellen, watching helplessly from the top of her ladder on the opposite side of the front porch, said sharply, "Ethan Hunter, if you won't cooperate, I'll finish the job alone!"

She regretted the tone the moment the words were out of her mouth. She hadn't the right to admonish him, and she was sure he'd be affronted.

But he'd simply climbed down the ladder, moved it, climbed up again, and said with a half smile, "My middle name is Bennett. If you're going to sound like a mother, you're supposed to use it."

SCHOOL WAS CANCELED on Monday because of the snow.

Travis stared gloomily out the window. "Dad won't be able to get home this afternoon," he said.

Ethan, standing behind him, put a hand on his shoulder. "It's okay. He'll just get a hotel room in Hartford or something. He'll be fine."

"How do you know?"

"Didn't you hear Kellen? He's going to live to see your children. Though I can't imagine any girl will ever want to marry you, you're such a weenie."

Travis turned around, small fists raised, and Kellen hurried toward them before violence could develop.

"Come on." She took a boy by each hand and sent them for their coats. "Let's put that energy to good use. Mom, come on. Mrs. Gibbons, get your coat."

"What?" She looked up from a pot of chili.

"Put that on low," she ordered, turning the knob on the stove herself and physically tugging the woman away from her duties. "Get your coat. We're going tobogganing."

"What?" The question had a more frantic quality this time as they all shrugged into outdoor gear.

"I saw two toboggans in the garage, and there's a nifty hill at the back of the house."

"But the..." Mrs. Gibbons pointed helplessly toward the stove as Kellen pushed her toward the door, pulling her mother along at the same time.

"Darling, I'm not sure my Medicare supplement is paid up," Mary Ellen protested, dragging her feet. Travis put his hands to her back and pushed.

"Mother, you're not old enough for Medicare."

"A week in your company and I find myself aging quickly. You're sure this is a good idea? My bones are brittle, you know. I never drank milk faithfully, and I smoked for several years while..."

Her protests went on as Kellen dispatched the boys to the garage for the toboggans, then led everyone up the slope at the back of the house.

"Sweetie, I know you hate to be psychoanalyzed," Mary Ellen said as the boys fell back to help Mrs. Gibbons. "But there's a certain frantic quality about your need to keep busy. It couldn't be that you're missing Dominic, could it?"

Kellen turned a stern gaze on her. "Don't," she said, "unless you want to be the one to make the test run."

Mary Ellen sighed and frowned at her. "Love makes most people happy. It's made you King Kong in a country-Christmas frenzy."

"That's it!" Kellen cried. "Get in a toboggan."

Two hours after Dominic had been due to arrive home, Kellen called the airport to check on the status of his flight. It had arrived. Then she called the hotel where Ethan said he usually stayed when he flew into Hartford too late to drive home. He wasn't registered.

"He probably went to dinner first," she said, suppressing her own concern to convince the boys that all was well.

"Wouldn't they have given him something to eat on the plane?" Travis asked.

Ethan shook his head. "Too short a flight."

An hour later, Travis pleaded with her to call the hotel again.

When they learned he still wasn't registered, Travis suggested, "Maybe he went to another hotel."

Kellen hugged him. "Maybe. But we can't call them all. I'm sure he'll be home as quickly as he can, but he'll probably have to wait until morning."

Kellen finally put a protesting Travis to bed at ten-thirty.

"Did you turn on the Christmas lights?" he asked, the question stopping her in the doorway. "I mean, in case he got stuck on the road and tried to walk home or something?"

"I'll do that right now," she promised. Then she went across the hall to check on Ethan, who lay staring at the ceiling, his hands folded behind his head.

"He's fine, Ethan," she said, tugging his covers up because she didn't know what else to do for him. "I'm sure of it."

"Then why hasn't he called?" he asked. "He always calls if he has a change of plans, or he's going to be late."

"I don't know," she replied after searching her mind for a plausible excuse. "But I'm sure he has a good reason."

"Yeah." His tone was skeptical as he turned onto his side, a tense set to the line of his shoulder.

The house was quiet, everyone else in bed, as Kellen flipped the switch that turned the house into a marquee for the approaching season. Then she poured a cup of coffee and went to sit by the window.

Finally alone with nothing else to do, she let the worry that had plagued her all evening take the place it wanted in the forefront of her mind. Unfortunately it didn't replace, but only magnified, her loneliness.

She was supposed to go home tomorrow, but she'd experienced life without him for the past few days and she knew without a fraction of a doubt that she far preferred life *with* him. In fact, she seemed incapable of even imagining a future without him and the boys. But she still couldn't quite believe that they could take the elements of their storybook encounter and adventure and make real life out of them. It seemed as impossible as leaving him did. What she needed, she thought with gallows humor, was an alternative that had possibilities.

"So, how are you holding up?" Her mother appeared, steaming cup of coffee in hand, to curl up in the corner of the sofa closest to Kellen. She wore a pale pink Mandarin-style robe she'd bought the day they went shopping.

Kellen forced a look of mild surprise, as though she'd no idea what she was talking about. "Fine. How are you?"

Mary Ellen balanced her cup on the arm of the sofa and gave her a level look.

"Kell, this is your mother you're speaking to. You don't have to be brave for me. Why don't you admit that you love Dominic, and you're worried about him?"

"Of course I'm worried about him," Kellen admitted. "Aren't you?"

"Yes, but because he's a very nice man, because he, with a little help from you, saved us all from being killed, and because I like his kids and want them all to be happy for a long, long time." She paused significantly. "Not because I spent several desperate days with him and now find myself deeply in love."

Kellen rose out of her chair and went to the fireplace to poke the fire that was burning just fine without help from her.

"Please," she said quietly. "You're not helping."

"I want to, Kellen," her mother said gravely. "Tell me what's wrong. What's holding you back from this?"

"I'm not—" She tried to deny, but she was interrupted.

"You're supposed to be at an age when you no longer believe your mother to be stupid. I saw it in you the night I crawled in through your window. You're so in love that you glow. But you're holding something back, and I know the word's grossly overworked, but it looks like commitment to me."

"Mother . . ."

"Why? Why are you doing this?"

Kellen spun around, sick with worry and indecision and her mother's unwillingness to be ignored.

"Because I don't want to be as unhappy as you were! Because I don't want to make the boys unhappy!"

A long moment of heavy silence filled the room. The fire crackled and the wind blew. Then Mary Ellen put her cup down, unfolded from the sofa, and went to Kellen.

"You mean because of the divorce?" Mary Ellen asked, clearly surprised.

"Yes." Kellen sank onto the bench on the stone hearth, remembering that time so clearly. "You were so unhappy, and so was I. I'm sure Daddy was, too. But it's more than that. You had the same kind of thing, you know. You fell in love with a storybook hero. It's just that yours was a cowboy and mine is a prince."

Momentarily distracted, Mary Ellen asked, "A prince?"

Kellen sighed. "Before I knew who he was I thought he was an exiled prince or something equally romantic. My point is that when it came to day-to-day living, your fairy tale didn't hold up."

Mary Ellen made an indignant little sound. "How dare you dismiss my marriage by saying it didn't 'hold up'. The love did, we just couldn't reconcile your father's need to be miles away from civilization, and mine to be in the thick of it, traveling from place to place to see what was new. But you're not up against anything like that, anyway. Who wouldn't be happy in this wonderful place?"

Kellen looked up at her wearily. "Mom, people chase him down, he gets shot at."

Mary Ellen shrugged. "That happened once. And you not only survived the situation, you emerged from it with a sparkle I've never seen in you before. Kell, please don't leave this relationship because you're afraid of what happened to your father and me."

Kellen stood, restless and anguished. "Mom, what happened to me might have been outlined by a screenwriter. It should be committed to celluloid, or disk or whatever they film with now. It's hard to believe it can be an introduction to a real life together."

Mary Ellen caught both her hands and held them. "Now listen to me," she said in maternal tones Kellen remembered very well from her childhood. "Close your eyes."

"Mom . . ."

"Do it. Close your eyes."

With a groan of exasperation, Kellen complied.

"Now clear your mind of everything but what you're feeling."

Kellen didn't find it difficult. What she felt was so pervasive.

Mary Ellen squeezed her hands. "Don't tell me what it is, but concentrate on it, trace it back to its cause, and tell me that you've ever felt anything more real than what you feel at this moment."

Kellen's eyes snapped open as she came to the realization instantly. What she felt was a complex mixture of dreadful worry and serious pain. The first was because she had no idea if Dominic was safe or not, and the second because she loved him desperately and it would tear her apart to leave him and the boys—or to lose them.

She put a hand to her stomach where the emotions churned and burned with very real pain.

She looked at her mother in astonishment that her complex confusion could have been so easily untangled.

Mary Ellen patted her cheek and walked away. "Good night, darling. Wake me if you hear anything."

Kellen stood for a long time in the middle of the room as layers of self-defense fell away and love wrapped around her, warm and adherent and, considering the circumstances, only a little comforting.

She wondered where Dandy was. She could use a friend right about now. She closed her eyes and began to pray for all she was worth.

IT WAS TWO O'CLOCK when she heard the roar. It startled her out of a doze, loud and rumbling and completely unidentifiable. It reminded her of the incident with the motorcycle in the tunnel. She went to the window, praying she and Dominic would have the chance to laugh over that again one day.

A strange pattern of lights in the distance caused a leap of hope in her chest. She opened the door and stepped out onto the porch, ignoring the frigid wind that swept around her and lifted her hair.

The lights came closer and she ran across the lawn to the driveway. The lights stopped where the road turned onto the drive. She ran halfway down it before she identified the vehicle as a snowplow. Her heart sank to her toes with an almost audible thud.

Then, in the glow of the headlights, she saw a figure leap down. There was the sound of conversation she couldn't decipher, then the snowplow lifted its blade, turned back onto the road and started away.

Kellen took several hesitant steps forward, wondering if she'd imagined that figure. Without the snowplow's lights, this end of the drive was in darkness, but she heard the unmistakable crunch of footsteps on snow.

Her heart leapt again, lodging in her throat. But it didn't prevent her from shouting.

"Dominic!"

"Kellen?" She heard his surprise on the frigid air. "Where are you? What are you . . . ? Kellen!"

She came, airborne, out of the swirling snow straight into his arms so that he had to drop his bag and briefcase and brace himself. She was sobbing and laughing and clinging to his neck, kissing him and saying things that made him believe he was rummy with exhaustion.

Then he realized that despite her unbridled affection, she felt like a glacier in his arms. He held her away to see that she was wearing the white outfit that had stopped him in his tracks the day he'd taken her and her mother shopping.

He pulled off his lined trenchcoat and wrapped it around her, pulling her back to him and enfolding her in his arms, rubbing her back to try to put warmth into her.

"What is the matter with you?" he demanded. "Do you want to catch pneumonia?"

"I love you," she said simply, burrowing against him.

He melted, despite the arctic wind blowing around them.

He held her another moment, wondering if his absence had truly been the clever move he'd hoped it would be, or if something had happened while he was gone. Then he turned her toward the house.

"Come on," he said, setting a quick pace, half carrying her with him as he hurried.

"What the...?" He hesitated as a square of bright lights appeared out of the snowy darkness.

"We decorated for Christmas," she said, kissing him again. "Do you like it? Wait till you see inside. But the boys insisted we wait for you to get the tree."

She tugged on him and he continued up the walk, the light-trimmed house blooming out of the blizzard like some arctic mirage. She'd even trimmed the dormers and the chimney. The sight melted the loneliness of the last few days but didn't completely smooth away the ache. Was she just relieved that he was safe? Or did this mean something else?

On the porch he was literally assaulted by his children, by Mrs. Gibbons and Mary Ellen.

While Travis hung from his neck, Ethan helped Kellen inside, the women flung a blanket around him and offered a scolding in tandem about people who wandered around in the snow and worried other people to death.

"Cool!" Travis enthused, making himself comfortable on Dominic's knee as Mrs. Gibbons sat him on the stone hearth. "You got to ride in a snowplow!"

Beside him, Kellen tucked her arm in his and sat as close as she could without climbing into his lap.

Mrs. Gibbons forced hot coffee into their hands. "We were worried sick about you. Why didn't you just wait until tomorrow?"

He smiled at Kellen, then winked at his boys. "Because I wanted to come home tonight. And the plow was coming my way, so I took the chance. It was slow going, but . . ." He looked down at the woman who'd been on his mind for three solid days and nights and saw the love in her eyes that had been there in his dream. "It got me here."

She squeezed his arm and leaned her cheek against his shoulder.

"Look at what we did!" Travis said excitedly, pointing to the garlanded stairway and the mantel. "And we fixed up Mom's old wreath and put it back on the bedroom door. Want to see?"

Mrs. Gibbons and Mary Ellen went arm in arm, whispering, into the kitchen, while he and Kellen and the boys paraded past the stairs to the bedroom.

Travis pointed proudly. "Isn't it beautiful?"

Dominic thought it was. It looked like the old wreath, but with new embellishments. It seemed to say to him everything he felt inside. Same old life, with wonderful new pieces that sparkled and shined.

Kellen held her breath. Had she taken too many liberties? Did he still feel the way he'd felt Thanksgiving night? Or had he had time to think over all her retreats and denials and decide she was a poor risk, after all?

He smiled down at Kellen. "It is beautiful. Thank you for putting it there."

She stared at him, trying to read between the lines. He studied her, trying to see into the glow she wore and decide what it meant.

"Umm...Trav?" Ethan turned his brother toward the stairs. "I think we should go to bed."

Travis looked at him as though he'd suggested they kiss girls. "But we don't have our presents yet. We always get presents."

Ethan kept pushing him. "We can wait till tomorrow."

"What?" Travis demanded. "I can't wait till tomorrow. I have to..."

Dominic wasn't sure how it had happened, but Kellen was in his arms, still staring into his eyes.

He pointed toward the living room and his bag without moving. "Front zipper pocket."

"You are so *stupid!*" Ethan was telling Travis as they hurried away.

"So, what does it mean?" Dominic asked, tilting his head to the side as she stood on tiptoe to nibble along his neck, apparently destined for his ear. Sensation both enervated and crippled him.

"What does...what mean?" she whispered. She had reached his earlobe and took it between her teeth.

The nip was deliciously painful.

"Everything," he said. "That...that greeting, the decorations..." He was having difficulty concentrating and this was important. He finally took hold of her shoulders and pulled her away, dredging up a look of firmness and pinning her with it. "The wreath. What does it mean?"

She seemed surprised. "It means I love you."

He nodded. "I knew you loved me when I left. What does it mean beyond that?"

There was no better way than the direct approach. But he looked just a little severe, and she wondered if it meant he really wanted the truth, or he was tired of her vacillation.

"It means," she said on a gusty breath, "that I want to stay if *you* still want *me*. That I love the boys and I love the dog and I love this house and, most important, I'm miserable when you're not with me."

Dominic took the first easy breath he'd drawn since the day he'd met her. She was his, and, finally, he wasn't the only one who knew it.

"Oh, I want you," he said, pulling her back into his arms with a fervor she couldn't mistake. "We'll get married next week. You can decorate windows in Connecticut instead of Oregon."

"Yes." She was delirious with joy. She'd have agreed to decorate windows in Abu Dhabi.

He removed one arm from around her to open the bedroom door.

"Well, I'll be damned," he said with a soft laugh.

She raised her head from his shoulder to look. Curled up in the middle of the bed was Dandy. And curled up against her, in the tight curve of nose to feet, was the fat orange blob of Carrot's body.

Dominic shook his head. "They made friends at last."

Kellen, her arms still wrapped around his middle, squeezed and allowed herself the luxury of possession and rubbed her cheek against his shoulder. "Some of us are a little slow."

He closed the door behind him, lifted her against him so that she could feel how much he needed her, and walked her toward the sofa in his office.

"Slow can be good," he whispered. "Very, very good."

Meet four of the most mysterious, magical men...in

In March, make a date with Daniel...

Suzanna Molloy had long been on the trail of the elusive Dr. Daniel Crompton. But when a chemical accident gave him fantastical powers, Suzanna found herself on the run...with a man who could become invisible and kiss her unawares, and whose fiery eyes could reduce objects—and Suzanna's resistance—to sizzling cinders. For Dr. Daniel Crompton had just become the gorgeous Cinderman....

Join Anne Stuart for

#525 CINDERMAN
March 1994

Don't miss any of the MORE THAN MEN titles!

Available wherever Harlequin books are sold.

SUPH4

Take 4 bestselling love stories FREE

Plus get a FREE surprise gift!

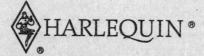

When the only time you have for yourself is...

Spring into spring—by giving yourself a March Break! Take a few *stolen moments* and treat yourself to a Great Escape. Relax with one of our brand-new stories (or with all six!).

Each STOLEN MOMENTS title in our Great Escapes collection is a complete and never-before-published *short* novel. These contemporary romances are 96 pages long—the perfect length for the busy woman of the nineties!

Look for Great Escapes in our Stolen Moments display this March!

SIZZLE by Jennifer Crusie
ANNIVERSARY WALTZ
by Anne Marie Duquette
MAGGIE AND HER COLONEL
by Merline Lovelace
PRAIRIE SUMMER by Alina Roberts
THE SUGAR CUP by Annie Sims
LOVE ME NOT by Barbara Stewart

Wherever Harlequin and Silhouette books are sold.

SMGE

HARLEQUIN®

Don't miss these Harlequin favorites by some of our most distinguished authors!
And now, you can receive a discount by ordering two or more titles!

HT#25409	THE NIGHT IN SHINING ARMOR by JoAnn Ross	$2.99	☐
HT#25471	LOVESTORM by JoAnn Ross	$2.99	☐
HP#11463	THE WEDDING by Emma Darcy	$2.89	☐
HP#11592	THE LAST GRAND PASSION by Emma Darcy	$2.99	☐
HR#03188	DOUBLY DELICIOUS by Emma Goldrick	$2.89	☐
HR#03248	SAFE IN MY HEART by Leigh Michaels	$2.89	☐
HS#70464	CHILDREN OF THE HEART by Sally Garrett	$3.25	☐
HS#70524	STRING OF MIRACLES by Sally Garrett	$3.39	☐
HS#70500	THE SILENCE OF MIDNIGHT by Karen Young	$3.39	☐
HI#22178	SCHOOL FOR SPIES by Vickie York	$2.79	☐
HI#22212	DANGEROUS VINTAGE by Laura Pender	$2.89	☐
HI#22219	TORCH JOB by Patricia Rosemoor	$2.89	☐
HAR#16459	MACKENZIE'S BABY by Anne McAllister	$3.39	☐
HAR#16466	A COWBOY FOR CHRISTMAS by Anne McAllister	$3.39	☐
HAR#16462	THE PIRATE AND HIS LADY by Margaret St. George	$3.39	☐
HAR#16477	THE LAST REAL MAN by Rebecca Flanders	$3.39	☐
HH#28704	A CORNER OF HEAVEN by Theresa Michaels	$3.99	☐
HH#28707	LIGHT ON THE MOUNTAIN by Maura Seger	$3.99	☐

Harlequin Promotional Titles

#83247	YESTERDAY COMES TOMORROW by Rebecca Flanders	$4.99	☐
#83257	MY VALENTINE 1993	$4.99	☐
	(short-story collection featuring Anne Stuart, Judith Arnold, Anne McAllister, Linda Randall Wisdom)		

(limited quantities available on certain titles)

	AMOUNT	$
DEDUCT:	10% DISCOUNT FOR 2+ BOOKS	$
ADD:	POSTAGE & HANDLING	$
	($1.00 for one book, 50¢ for each additional)	
	APPLICABLE TAXES*	$ _____
	TOTAL PAYABLE	$ _____
	(check or money order—please do not send cash)	

To order, complete this form and send it, along with a check or money order for the total above, payable to Harlequin Books, to: **In the U.S.:** 3010 Walden Avenue, P.O. Box 9047, Buffalo, NY 14269-9047; **In Canada:** P.O. Box 613, Fort Erie, Ontario, L2A 5X3.

Name: _____

Address: _____ City: _____

State/Prov.: _____ Zip/Postal Code: _____

*New York residents remit applicable sales taxes.
 Canadian residents remit applicable GST and provincial taxes.

HBACK-JM